SUNSHINE BEAM PUBLISHING

Sunshine Beam Books are published by
Sunshine Beam Publishing Inc., Hollywood, CA 90072

Design by Anna Huff

First Printing, January 1993
Second Printing, March 1993

PRINTED IN THE U.S.A.

Slouchers

The Novelization

A Novel by
E.L. LESSERT

Based on the Screenplay by
MAC MCHENRY

SUNSHINE BEAM PUBLISHING

Credits

Director	JERROYLD HOLT
Screenwriter	MAC MCHENRY
Producer	JED ROGERS
Willow Montgomery	LISSA CHRISTENSSEN
Spooner	LAYTON HOLDDS
Vicky	STEPHANIE AGUILAR
Jack Jack	EMMET HYDE
Cody	DONEL GOULDING
Wes	ZAIRE ORLANDO
Skip	MICAH MILES
Toody	HUGH BOYD
Tabitha Soren	SELF
Dragon	SHANNON LINDER
Clove Cigarette Roller	JOMS
Kurt Cobain's Guitar Tech	BUZZY NECO
Matt Dillon's Wig Artist	JIMMY TOEM
Mopey Guy #1	AMELIE CANCO
Mopey Guy #2	JASON CORDEON
Mopey Guy #3	BRUCE L.
Amusing Man Who Makes Mopey Guys Laugh	TODD L.
Miss Soren's Hair Coloring	DAPHNE ELISABETH
Funny Muslim	AMER YAQUB
Air-Guitar Coach	ELAINE ZELDA LEVIN
Goatee Groomer	LUCIANNA ELLIE
Three Men, Standing in Triangle, Pointing Guns at Each Other	MIKE S., SCOTT J., JASON R.
Choreographer to "My Sharona"	MARK LARNICK
Poseur Tech	GERALD LEON
Heroin Addict #3	ELLIOT KORTMANN
Heroin Addict #23	GORDON CARTER
"Mister Flannel"	SUZANNE ROSEN
"Dr. Granola"	JONESEY
Hoops the Hawk	HOOPS THE HAWK
Rock Concert Scalper	TED TRAVELSTEAD
Swing Dancer #1	JENNI K.
Grunge Sweetheart	KATIE I.

Biking Shorts Over White Underwear.....TOMMY TOMERSON
Grunge Slang Advisor.. JACK JACKS
Lovin' Dat Muff... MATTHEW RYDER
Janeane Garofalo Wrangler...............................SKITCH LYNCH

Music.. MARK ROZZO
Lyrics..STEVE WILSON

Grunge Stylist ....PETER BALTRA
MTV Font Designer... ANNA HUFF

The filmmakers wish to thank the town and citizens of Seattle, Washington, as well as Yvonne Mendard, Monk Vintage, Winston Churchill High, Mayor Norman Blann Rice and Cup O' Joe for providing the "Go Go Juice to Get Up and Go Go"

Slouchers!

Tuesday, 3:35 P.M.

Imagine descending through those impenetrable, yeasty clouds and seeing below a city pulsating with youth. It could be Swinging London in the 1960s. Or Paris in the 1920s. San Francisco in the Summer of Love. EPCOT Centre in 1982. Keep floating down, past the towers, through the mist, and you will come to realize that this is the most exciting time in history to be young and alive. The rain-soaked streets vibrate with an intensity that can barely be described. There's anguish. Pain. All deliciously mixed into a sludgy gumboed sluice seasoned with a dash of dozy angst and a pinch of logy torment.

This is Seattle.

This is the early 1990s.

It is *exhilarating*.

Limitless, the possibilities.

Anything could happen b/c 90's

Keep floating, eventually to earth and to a parking lot next to a failing strip mall. Come to a stop before a young woman, so beautiful as to be almost fictional.

Except she is real.

No bigger than a wisp but sturdier than anything that could possibly stand in her way. More than merely beautiful ... beautifully *obtainable*. Her name is Willow.

And this is where our incredible story begins and will take place over the following astonishing two weeks:

1

Willow removes the lens cap from her <u>Fuji DS-100 digicam with 3-power zoom</u>. She hits the large POWER button (red, square) and turns the video camera on herself.

She narrates aloud for the benefit of her own camera:

"This is Willow Montgomery. I am twenty-three years old. I wasn't born in Seattle but I moved here *before* all the poseurs arrived. I'd like to introduce you to a few of my very best friends in the entire Seattle area. I would like to think we're all *incredibly* special. I think you will soon feel the same. This is a *revolution*! Start it off, Spooner! *Entertain us*!"

"Darth Vader was Paul," exclaims Spooner, slapping a street-hockey shot into a makeshift net fashioned from white tubing stolen from behind a medical supply store. The shot misses. The puck is a discarded wheel from an abandoned children's scooter.

Spooner rollerblades in a circle and pumps his fists much like the rollerblading champion he is. Or *wants* to be. His dream is to one day become the Rollerblading Champion of Seattle. It's Spooner's one way out of this parking lot. He doesn't know how else to escape this home he's created for himself, walled off by bustling roads and buttoned-up losers on their way to their white-collar McJobs.

To earn some loose change, Spooner works a few days a week as a messenger for important legal documents. Inside his bag now is an exceedingly serious document that needs to be delivered to an official in charge of the city's drinking water. It's from the mayor, himself, and has to do with pesticides or something that could be harmful to children and the aged or something or other. It's been in Spooner's bag for weeks.

He rollerblades into a perfect figure 4.

"R2 was Ringo. C3PO was their fey manager. And Han Solo, well, he was George," he goes on.

"More like '*Hand* Solo'," says Jack Jack, his rainbow-colored Jamaican tam bobbing with each stride powered by Lightning Freestyle black roller-blades, oversized laces in neon yellow. "If you catch my *smell*."   *Star Wars meant lots to people without*

Jack Jack doesn't work in the "traditional sense" *jobs* but does operate an illegal sensory-deprivation tank *in* behind the strip-mall—essentially an empty storage *early* unit filled to the top with tap water. Most customers *90s* enjoy it, imagining that they're far, far away in a land that's so much warmer and sunnier.

Some never make it out.

Jack Jack's biggest dream is to perform his conceptual one-person show, "Racism Manifesto, Part One," about The Rodney King situation, during a seventh inning stretch at the Seattle Kingdome. There's no reason why it can't happen. He knows someone who knows someone who knows the assistant marketing director for the Mariners.

"Because you jerk off," says Cody, seated on top of a garbage can, leisurely smoking an American Spirit taken from the Convenience Mart. He's wearing a 1920s newsboy cap. "We *get* it."

Cody manages the video store, open one hour a

3

day to rent movies featuring three male characters on the VHS cover, all in black trench coats, standing in a triangle, pointing a handgun at each other. It's incredibly cool.

There are hundreds of these particular movies to choose from. They are a "thing" this year.

Cody knows literally every detail about every movie ever made. He prefers the bad to the good. The Italian spaghetti westerns to the mainstream Hollywood hits. The bootlegged five-hour versions of comedies over the ninety minute versions of test-screened averageness. Cody hopes to one day attend film school and shoot ironic movies chock-full of references to previously shot movies.

"But who was John?" Cody asks.

"Greedo," Topper responds, zipping past on a longboard, jumping the curb with his LA Gear HAJ hightops, performing a 180 and nailing the landing. *Wicked.*

Topper owns Convenience Mart—unofficially called the In-Convenience Mart—located, inconveniently, just behind the video store. He works two hours a week selling plastic-bagged nourishments and libations that go well with marijuana, including the store's number one winner, Surge—Coke's powerful answer to Pepsi's Mountain Dew, advertised to have more of a "hardcore" edge.

Topper is known throughout Seattle as the "Rolling Paper Sommelier." For the past six years, he has consumed only stale nachos and melted cheeeeeezz, with six 'e's and two 'z's. His complexion reminds

Willow of a creature that might live within the deepest reaches of the Mariana Trench. *deepest part of worlds ocean*

Topper knows someone who knows someone who knows Eddie Vedder's personal assistant.

"Got another theory," says Cody, his shoulder-length green hair drenched in misty condensation. "Stu Sutcliffe was the uncle, the guy who died before his time. Never did live to see the success of the Rebel Force, the one he helped create with his own damn space money. *That* wasn't fair."

"Who'd be Jabba the Hut?" questions Topper, skateboarding past nonchalantly, sipping on a steaming cup of strong joe. He's showing off for the camera, not that Willow minds.

"Yoko," says Cody. *singer from 60's*

Cody, twenty-two, wears a 1970s era T-shirt with the Twinkie the Kid mascot emblazed across it.

Over that, he wears a black tux vest.

He's found this outfit where he finds *all* his clothes: at the second-hand store that sells apparel with 1970s food mascots emblazoned on them. Yesterday he wore a T-shirt with the Kool-Aid Pitcher Man bursting through the Berlin Wall, holding a sign reading: "Will Work For Food!!"

It was very funny and Cody received many half-approving nods.

"Did you guys know R2D2 and C3PO were designed by the same inventor?" announces Cody. "But that he was bi-polar? So each robot represents a *different* emotional side to his personality?"

"Watched *Jaws* again last night," says a voice from

the pitched roof, changing the subject.

It is Wes.

Willow's camera pans upwards, past the NO LOITERING SIGN. Wes likes to sit on roofs. Also, he is gay, which can only make Willow's documentary that much more interesting—and current. Homosexuals have been in the news recently because they are "coming out of the closet," which means they are announcing to their families they are "homosexuals."

This has never before happened in the history of "homosexuality," which most likely goes back years, if not decades. *True*

"I believe that the entire premise of *Jaws* was based on the Kennedy assassination," he finishes.

When Willow first met him, a week ago, Wes had already been on the roof for a month. *He's in it for the long haul!*

"Here we go," says Cody. He rolls his eyes in mock exasperation. He doesn't have time for any of this.

Actually, he does. *That's what slacker means.*
All he has, really, is time. *Time meant nothing.*

The video store doesn't open for another hour. It will then close one hour beyond that.

Cody likes to earn extra dough by participating in the bootleg cassette and video black market: celebrity sex tapes, illegal rock concert movies, and hours upon hours of hilarious bloopers from the recently released *Silence of the Lambs,* including a long scene in which the lotion is *not* properly placed in the basket.

Wes, up on the roof, also has nothing but time. He's been kicked out of his home and he intends to

6

stay up on the slanted roof until his parents, who just don't understand, eventually visit him and profusely apologize.

Like all parents in movies, they do not understand "homosexuals."

But Wes is a Gen X'er.

And Gen X'ers take matters into their *own* hands!

The term "Gen X" was coined in 1991 by writer and "Baby Boomer" Douglas Coupland. *this is true*

"Baby Boomer" is another important sociological term, this one coined years ago by a writer from the "Greatest Generation."

Before that, no generations—at least with any marketable names—ever existed.

That's just the way it was.

And this is the way it is *now* …

"Okay," says Wes, from the roof, encouraged. "So listen to this: the shark is Oswald, right? The first woman to be killed—the swimmer in the ocean—that would represent Kennedy, okay? The rest of the dead would be the soldiers in Vietnam, yeah?" Wes looks down at Willow. "Isn't the memory card full? You've been shooting for ten minutes already, right?"

"Not yet," answers Willow. "Few more minutes! Show the entire universe what you're made of!"

It's interesting that the Kennedy assassination was just mentioned. One of Willow's all-time cinematic influences—more so than even Truffaut, whom she has yet to see—is the herky-jerky camera movements from the *Zapruder Film*, so influential on MTV's documentarian, vérité style: exciting, loose, impulsive.

Volatile.

Standing gingerly, and making sure his left foot is planted properly so as to not fall off the roof, Wes spreads his arms wide. "Welcome to our reality! We've just graduated from college. And we have no jobs. Or prospects! Fuck it! *Down* the *up* elevator!"

As if to prove his point, Wes opens his graduation robe wide and dips his head so that his mortar board can be seen. It's badly stained with alcoholic drinks. Written in white electrical tape across it is "NOW! WHAT?!"

Beneath his robe, Wes wears a ripped T-shirt recently purchased from Old Navy. He would have ripped it himself, in all the right places, but he figured he'd just let the Chinese workers do it themselves.

"We call it our maxi pad," announces Topper to the world. "Our den of equality. Here, *anybody* is free to be a sloucher!"

"And *proud* of it," Cody semi-screams.

Cody slumbers over to the pay phone. He's holding a half-eaten slice and a stack of quarters. He places the receiver to his ear. He's been on hold forever with KQMV, the grunge radio station. He wants them— no, *needs* them—to play "Smells Like Teen Spirit."

It's been fifteen minutes.

Fuck it.

On to something new.

He hangs up. Inserts quarters. He dials 1-900-DAY-DREA.

An operator answers. "1-900-DAYDREAM. How

may I assist you to daydream today?"

"I need a daydream please," says Cody.

He'd think of one himself but he's too lazy.

"How old are you?"

"Twenty-three."

"Interests?"

"Films. Pop culture. Sci-fi. Um …"

He pauses. *What else?*

"Fantasy, I guess? Horror. That's about it. Oh, equal rights for … everyone, I guess, too?"

The operator is silent. She's thinking. *What would a twenty-three year old with these particular interests daydream about?*

"I think I have it," she eventually says. "You're a famous filmmaker. And you're walking into the premiere of your new blockbuster. It's all about monsters."

"I daydreamed that the other day. Another operator gave it to me."

"*Hmmmm.* Then let's try this one. You're attending a party with many beautiful women—do you like women?"

"Yes."

"Okay. A bevvy of beautiful women are attending a party and you are invited. Maybe you had a crush on a few in high school. Typically in these sorts of social situations, you're shy, you don't say much. Not that you *can't*. It's just that you don't *want to*. But you decide that *this* party will be *different*. You walk in confidently. All heads turn. You loudly announce that you have a few conspiracy theories about the movie

9

The Shining. There's a gasp. *What a way to enter a party! The women are stunned! They've never seen or heard anything like this*!"

"Oooh, that's *good*," says Cody. "Very good, yes! I *like* that!"

"Before long, the most beautiful women are in the bedroom, listening to all of your fascinating, *original* theories on *The Shining*."

"*Ooooh*."

"You have so many Stanley Kubrick theories, like how The Overlook's distinctive, hexagonally-patterned carpeting depicts the chemical compound for the son-to-be invented crack cocaine. The girls are blown away. They're in heaven. You sit back on the bed, your arms behind your head, and you're nodding, as if to say: *Yeah. No big deal. I just knew you would dig my theories. Whatever!*"

"Wow."

"And that is your daydream for today."

"Do I sleep with them?"

"I'm afraid you'll have to insert another $1.25 in quarters to find out."

Cody hangs up.

Harsh realm.

But cool. He can handle the rest of the daydream himself. He has enough to work with—*barely*, but enough. He takes a bite out of his pizza, a huge one. He places the slice back down on to the dirty, metallic surface within the phone booth. It'll be safe until he returns in ten minutes. He blades over to the curb, mouth stuffed, and sinks down with a loud sigh. His energy for the day is sapped.

But he has some daydreaming to do ...

"Hey, everyone!" says Topper, skateboarding past Cody, "how much realistically to run into the Convenience Mart right now, buck naked, and then eat a roller dog and then jet right back out? How much realistically would it take for you to do that? Seriously? *Realistically?*"

"Twenty," says Jack Jack.

"Fifteen," says Wes.

"I'd do it for *nothin'*," says Royce, chewing languidly on a straw. "Fuck it. I'd do *anything* for free. I'm *crazy* like *that!*" *Today would be called PTSD*

Royce smokes his Camels "straight." Kicked out of the Army after forcing the citizens of Baghdad to memorize at gunpoint the lyrics to R.E.M.'s "Everybody Hurts", he's back in Seattle and living it up in the parking lot. Royce is the badass of the bunch, the one with the streetwise panache. The one who wears the Army fatigues and a hospital bracelet that's never been explained but is now fraying. The bracelet is tie-dyed.

Sipping on a 40, Royce has just returned from yet another visit to the plasma bank. His purpose this time was to pay for all the personal lubrication at the Convenience Mart that will assist him in making a deposit at the sperm bank so that he can earn enough money for all the Ring Dings and tall cans of 40 he so desperately craves at the Convenience Mart.

It's the *perfect* hustle.

"Then why *don't* you?"

Royce shrugs. He adjusts his camouflage Army

11

jacket. He fiddles with his plastic hospital bracelet.

"Juss don't feel like it, is all," he says. "Fuck it. Fuck *everything*!"

"Hey, guys," asks Topper. "Can I ask you a personal question?"

"Sure," says Wes from the roof.

"So when you're sitting in a pool and you feel something that ain't cool, does it *have* to be diarrhea?"

Wes laughs. He's heard this before. And yet it never grows tiresome.

Willow turns off her video cam by hitting the large, red STOP button.

"You guys," announces Willow. "Incredible! *Amazing*! MTV will *love* this! You guys are the best! Just acting like yourselves, you're *stars*! The world will soon know you *all*!"

"When's the contest deadline?" asks Wes, sitting back down on the roof's slope, making room for his graduation robe to bloom out like a red cloud within a heroin syringe. "When do you have to mail this in?"

Leave it to the homosexual character to be overly concerned about logistics!

"One week from today," answers Willow. "At *exactly* this time. They'll pick a winner, live on the air, for their *Voice of a Generation*! I'm going to be cutting it *close*! But I *must* get this right, I just *have* to! There are no *second* chances!"

"And then you'll be MTV's first *Grunge Veejay*!" says Topper, skateboarding past, sipping on a mug of locally crafted Hefferveisen brew, the latest hops "craze."

There are so many breweries in this Northwest city that you can practically smell yeast in the air!

Willow prays it's yeast.

"And we can all move into your mansion. And do nothing *all* day, *every* day," exclaims Topper.

"*Do?*" asks Jack Jack. "More like yabba-dabba-*don't!*"

"I thought you wanted to be the first skateboarder to perform a 360-inward-double-heelflip in slow motion on a Doritos TV ad," says Wes.

Topper's face flushes. That is, indeed, his dream. But when someone else says it, it just sounds too insurmountable for anyone to actually achieve …

"Maybe," he mumbles. "I don't know. You know, *maybe*."

"I don't want to be MTV's first grunge veejay," says Willow. "I want to be a *filmmaker*. I want to capture my *generation* on expensive VHS tape."

"But can we still move into your mansion? And do nothing all day, every day?" asks Topper. "When you get famous?"

"We do that anyway," says Wes from above. "All day, every day. *Nothing*."

"Right. But we can then do it *inside*," says Topper. "And not *outside*. Where it rains."

"Rain is nothing but a conceit," announces Wes.

"Of what?"

"Of *reality*," says Wes. "We're living within a giant computer."

"Like *Tron*?" asks Topper, reaching for another nacho and dipping it into a cardboard container of liquid cheese. "Greed is *good*. Nachos are *better*."

"Can you imagine?" asks Topper. "We're nothing more than images and pictures inside a huge Tandy TRS-80 in the sky?"

"Can't even," says Cody, although it's hard to tell if he's being sarcastic.

"Being programmed by a Radio Shack employee to do *anything* the guy wants," says Topper.

"So you're saying that if my programmer wants me to spit, then he would just have me spit?" asks Jack Jack.

He spits.

"Yes."

"But what if my programmer does *not* want me to spit and yet *I* want to spit?"

Jack Jack goes to spit but stops himself at the last moment.

"Then he *never* wanted you to spit," says Cody. "He didn't want you to spit from the *beginning*."

Jack Jack spits.

"I guess he *did* want you to spit. So he just *had* you do it."

Jack Jack spits.

"*Wanted* you to spit."

Jack Jack goes to spit, stops himself.

"*Didn't* want you to spit."

"So what you're saying," says Jack Jack, "is that I have zero sovereignty over my own destiny?"

"*You vill obey the programmer's wishes or zelse!*" says Wes, from the roof, in the voice of Sergeant Schultz from *Hogan's Heroes*.

14

"All this with an 8-bit Radio Shack computer," says Topper. "Imagine the possibilities with a *16-bit*!"

"But if we all are truly and really programmed," says Spooner to Wes, "would this mean you were programmed to be gay?"

"Wouldn't want it any other way," says Wes, now in his own voice.

"*I'm a Pepper, he's a Pepper, she's a Pepper, wouldn't you like to be a Pepper, too?*" sings Spooner, mimicking the 1970s Dr. Pepper commercial he sings whenever something even halfway earnest is said in conversation.

The Greatest Generation had their earnestness.

The Gen X'ers have something far better: *studied insouciance*.

Something that actually *matters*.

"You might be a Pepper but crass materialism will get you nowhere," declares Cody, sipping from a plastic bottle of OK Cola. He is obsessed with this drink, as are all twenty-somethings.

The Greatest Generation had their World War II.

The Gen X'ers have something far better: the Cola Wars.

"Time to hit the grindstone," declares Willow, as she clips the digicam onto a belt-loop of her factory-aged work jeans, just next to her large pink beeper. "Can't just *chat* all day!"

"You'll know where to find us," Wes announces from behind her, still on the roof. "Out here, in our little slice of paved heaven."

Cody is at the curb. He's done with his daydream.

15

He didn't end up sleeping with any of the beautiful women after talking about conspiracy theories from *The Shining* but he did manage to receive oral pleasure.

So, really, the daydream could have been a hell of a lot worse.

"Yeah, ain't going nowhere," agrees Topper, still on top of the overturned trash can. "Because there ain't *nowhere* to go."

"Turtle and the hare," says Jack Jack. "Turtle and the hare."

"Prozac and the booze," says Wes. "Prozac and the booze." joking... no such fable exists

"Echoing that," says Cody, mouth full of 'za, some of which falls to the concrete below. "Man, remember when twenty-two felt old?! Now it don't feel like nothin'!"

"Rimbaud did he best work *before* twenty," says Spooner. "Maybe we're doomed."

He lazily scratches at his club hand-stamp. It is in the shape of Bart Simpson wearing unlaced combat boots. Cody is infamous for being too cool to chew; and when he's *truly* feeling the grunge spirit—too lazy to even breathe—he'll wear a working sleep apnea mask fashioned for the daytime. The mask is flanneled.

"It's the nineties," Jack Jack says, as way of explanation. "It's the motherfuckin' nineties."

"See ya soon, boys," says Willow, leaving the parking lot and the amazing conversation behind.

She enters a record store.

The bells above the door's entrance jingle-jangle out the opening notes to Talking Head's "Burning Down the House."

At the counter, as always, stands Skip.

Skip, the owner and boss of Number One Vinyl Xperience, is cantankerous, irritable, grouchy, and yet full of potential love. He's not so bad once you manage to crawl beneath his scaly, psoriasis-baked, alterna veneer.

He adores music of all kinds, as long as it's "fucking good," but still prefers "progressive, left of the dial" to any other musical genre. He hasn't yet quite come around to "grunge."

Skip is a Sonic Youth completist.

Skip owns the only flexi-disc of The Residents "Unlistenable 45" in the entire western hemisphere.

Skip is the king of the Cassette Underground. He prefers Elliott Murphy to Bruce Springsteen, Richard Verlaine to Fleetwood Mac, Jobriath to David Bowie, the Shins to the Beatles. College radio isn't progressive enough for him.

Only illegal, pirate radio will do.

Willow, who works as the store's assistant manager, and has done so for three days now, hopes to switch up Skip's taste a bit. Sometimes all it takes is just the tiniest hint of a "nudge grunge."

"Back from Never Never Land, Tinker Bell?" Skip asks. "How're the Lost Boys? Lost now and forever?"

Skip is twenty-nine and looks like a cross between Frank Black and Stephen Malkmus, with a dash of the wall-eyed lead singer from Radiohead thrown in for good measure.

Or just measure.

Ignoring him, Willow makes her way to the small back office. Once there, she takes a quick glance around. It's just as she had left it ten minutes earlier: Covered floor to ceiling with that perfect amount of music-related chaos: concert-ticket stubs pinned to corkboards; promotional album sleeves from local bands with names that sound familiar but not overly; an extremely hilarious and funny rubber chicken nailed above the bathroom door; a map of the United States with each state's best alternative band high-lighted with a brightly colored push-pin; and stacks of cassettes and LPs leaning this way and that; a dog in the corner, sleeping.

This is Toby the Wonder Pooch, who provides comic relief to the workers and customers by being dressed each morning as a different character from a 1970s sitcom.

Toby is dressed today as "Alice," so named for the lovable maid from *The Brady Bunch.* Yesterday, it was Schneider, the janitor from *One Day at a Time.* The day before, he was Mrs. Brady's gynecologist, Dr. Levetstein, the only Semite to ever appear on the show.

Willow picks up the phone and dials her own home number. When her answering machine picks up between the third and fourth rings, she presses the # key and punches in "1234." She waits to hear if anyone has left a message. They haven't. She hangs up. She does this about thirty to forty times a day.

Through the office window, Willow notices a few customers in the Heavy Metal area, a few nobodies hair-sprayed back to 1987, woozedly raking through the latest and tired releases from Warrant, Extreme, Poison, Wargasm.

Wouldn't know musical quality if it bit 'em on their suburban, pathetic asses!

"Okay, new list," screams Skip, from the counter. He clears his throat. This one is *important*.

"Top five songs to listen to as you masturbate into a black dress sock!"

Skip, like most adult men over a certain age, enjoys making lists that no one particularly enjoys hearing. Skip prefers this to actual sexual intercourse with a live female.

"Couldn't help you there," says Willow, making her way over to the front register and closer to Skip. She cinches the flannel shirt around her waist. Her "shit kickers"—the term for her unlaced Doc Martens—skuffle unhurriedly beneath her. The videocamera is still clipped to her jeans, just in case. gaucho is cowboy

Like a gaucho with a six-shooter. in spanish

"Not asking for any help," says Skip. "Let's start with the obvious. 'Crazy Rhythms" by the Feelies. That's a non-starter. Where to now? Well, you can't *not* have Joy Division, right? So let's go with 'Atmosphere.'"

"This all sounds very familiar to your top five songs to listen to after you masturbate into a *paper bag*," says Willow.

"*Totally* different," responds Skip. "A completely

different mood created for each setting. I picture the jack-off sock as more of an afternoon event. An 'Afternoon Delight,' as you were. The paper bag is more of a night time receptacle. So perhaps 'Golden Brown' by the Stranglers for the sock. And … 'Bittersweet' off the second Hoodoo Gurus album for the paper bag."

"Why don't you stop making lists and start making love?" Willow asks.

"Don't believe in love," says Skip. "No time for it. Besides, I'm too busy re-organizing my record collection."

"In what order this time?" asks Willow, sighing.

Skip feels the deep urge to re-order his records three or four times a week.

"Societal importance."

"How long will it take for this particular re-org?"

"Hopefully the rest of my life."

He smiles. He *means* it.

"What was the time before?"

"Purchase date."

"And before that?"

"Before that …" Skip mentally tabulates the list in his head. "Bassists who thumb slap. Before that: the worth of the albums on the black market, then by genre, then by alphabetical order by the city in which the LP was mastered, then by how much I paid for them, then by how much the *previous* owner paid for them, then by how much the future owner *will* pay for them, and then a very personal method of which only I can understand."

"Which would be what?"

"Secret."

"C'mon."

"Okay. I organize them according to the records that I've actually listened to and not just fondled while nude on my twin bed." His head drops. "I have over 10,000."

"So how many have you actually *listened* to?"

"Two hundred?"

"And how many have you ever listened to with *another* person?"

Skip is silent. "The fun is in the reorganizing," he mumbles.

The bells above the front door chime "Bad-da-da-da-dum. Badum. Ba. *Bum*."

A man enters, close to Willow in age, yet clearly lower on the Alternative IQ scale:

A real straight arrow, decked out like a working monkey. Tired suit, polished Thom McAn indoor-mall shoes. A yuppie nine-to-fiver who more than likely owns his own car, a "cager" with his own actual checking account. Super *ambitious*. A pencil pusher who remains confined—and *happily*—within the cubicled prison of his own pathetic existence.

"Watch *this*," announces Skip in a high voice, narrating his own version of what is about to take place. "Um, like, geez … um, do you have this album that I just heard on the classic rock radio station …"

The man, necktie as straight as his bearing, steps up to the counter. He is new to this world. To Willow and Skip, he seems dressed in an entirely different language.

He eyes Willow for a moment longer than necessary. His attention turns back to Skip. His brow furrows in deep concentration. It looks as if he is about to recite pi to the thousandth numeral.

"So, um, there's this song," he begins. "I heard it on the classic rock station."

Where did this creature come from?

Skip shoots Willow a look. *Here we go ...*

"The band begins with an A? As if it's a guy's name? Like Aaron Smith or something?"

"That would be *Aerosmith*," corrects Skip. "And you probably heard 'Dream On' or 'Walk This Way.'"

"Yes! 'Dream On'," says the man, eyes aglow with excitement. "To be honest, I'm not all that into music but ... *wow*! *What a song*!"

Skip sighs. He has no time for uppity straights who dig the cob-nobblin' Classic Rock. Classic *Alternative*, yes. But Classic Rock is a waste of time, a genre best left to the awful Boomers, aging hippies who rutted and procreated like forest creatures knee-deep in the fecund Woodstock mud.

With a slight, annoyed wave of his hand, Skip motions over to the compact disc aisle. Thankfully, there is only one aisle of CDs and, praise god, it's a tiny one. "Go buy your tinny music on shitty inferior discs, okay? Leave the *fuller, richer* experience to the rest of us *vinyl* lovers. The sound is *thicker*."

"C'mere," says Willow, who agrees with Skip but is a lot more patient with rock neophytes who don't know their <u>Nirvana '92s</u> from their <u>Nirvana '65s</u>.

She leads the customer over to the appropriate

real band called Nirvana **22**
in England in 60s

aisle. There is a hand-drawn sign hanging above with a green poison face, tongue out, two Xs for eyes.

"What's *his* problem?" asks the straight.

At first Willow thinks he's referring to Mr. Yuk, the green poisonous character, but he isn't.

Just Skip.

"Shouldn't that guy be happy that I'm in his place, spending money? I mean, this store ain't the biggest commerce success in town, right? Is he high or something?"

Willow laughs. "You're one of those capitalist lovers," she declares.

"Capitalist lovers?"

"The world is so much *more* than only commerce," she patiently explains.

Willow, not long ago, was also a rat chasing a cube of cheese in a maze that went on into eternity.

No longer.

"What does that mean?" asks Mr. Straight. "That the world is so much *more* than only commerce? What else could there be?"

"Like good taste," she says. "Not speaking of which, *here* you go."

Willow hands over the *Best Of Aerosmith* CD, gingerly holding it with her thumb and forefinger, as if toxic.

"Those who like classic rock don't have good taste?" Mr. Straight asks, taking the CD. He looks genuinely perplexed. He bites his lip.

"Let me ask you this," says Willow, tightening her flannel shirt around her waist even tighter. She doesn't know why she does this. It just feels right. Beyond that, everyone seems to be doing it lately. "What are you reading? Who's your favorite author?"

"Well, let's see. I enjoy … James Michener for fiction. Tom Clancy for non-fiction. And, um …"

"How about Hunter S. Thompson?" asks Willow. It comes out wearily although she didn't mean it to. "Or Charles Bukowski?"

"Never heard of them," says the straight. "Should I have?"

"Ever attended a concert?"

"Phil Collins in '85," he says. "I fucking love that song about the drowning that he witnessed but did nothing about. What an asshole!"

"Any festivals? Bumbershoot? Rock Against Reagan?"

"Just a few hours spent at Lollapalooza. My girl-friend at the time loved Luscious Jackson."

"Any desert-music happenings?"

"*Happenings*? I've never even been to the desert."

Willow smiles. There's just no reaching certain types. She herself hasn't read either of the authors' work she just mentioned but she definitely digs their most amazing philosophy. Burroughs, too. And Rimbaud. His photo hangs above her bed. She'll have to read some of their work one day.

"I adore them," she says. "Maybe you will, too. Depends on what you want out of life. Or what you *don't* want."

"What do you *not* want?" asks the straight.

"I don't know," says Willow coolly. "*What do*

24

you got?"

Toby the Wonder Pooch moseys over to Mr. Straight and barks.

"Nice dog," he says, a bit nervously.

"Toby," says Willow. "He's a good boy."

"Dressed as a *girl* dog, I see."

Willow rolls her eyes.

Hardly.

"Alice. From *Brady Bunch*."

"Oh," says Mr. Straight.

Toby barks again, louder.

"We have Brady Bunch re-enactment parties sometimes," continues Willow. "We read from actual scripts and make funny facial expressions. It's ironic and fun." *big thing in the early 90s*

"Okay," says Mr. Straight, not impressed.

The guy is impossible.

Willow takes the CD over to the cash register. "As for this winner, it'll be $11.99."

"Do you accept credit cards?" asks Mr. Straight, taking out his genuine leather wallet, no doubt purchased at an indoor mall's Banana Republic.

God, Willow thinks. *She should have known this mumblebutt wouldn't pay in cash! And that he'd be using a traditional wallet instead of a large rubber band stolen from the vegetable section of a grocery store!*

"No, but we do accept personal checks," she answers. "As long as you have a certified driver's license. Not everyone does. But I can see that *you* do."

Willow can't make out the exact age on the license

25

but she does see that it's been issued in California. And that the straight's name is Kevin. No surprise. He probably graduated business school and headed straight up to Seattle in order to take advantage of the *real* Seattle-ites like her.

Couldn't the marketers and bankers just leave her and her generation alone already?!

"Really? Is that true? That not everyone has a driver's license?" Mr. Straight asks, pulling out a $20 and placing it on the counter. "Then how do they get around?"

"There's a little something called *walking*," explains Willow, making change and handing it back. "Not to mention cycling. Would you like a bag?"

"I'm fine," Mr. Straight answers, taking the CD. "Well, thanks for the *interesting* chat. Learned a *lot*."

He's not being sarcastic. He *really* has learned a lot.

How suburban!

"Have a nice day, *sir*," says Skip, emphasizing "sir." "Please come back again, *soon*." He emphasizes "soon." Continuing, Skip says: "Or, better yet, just shop at the CD World in the indoor *mall*." He emphasizes "mall."

By this point, even Mr. Straight seems to be grasping the idea. *Emphasize the last word in a spoken sentence.* He looks as if he's about to respond, but only grins at Willow and walks out. The bells above the door chime in syncopated new-wave harmony.

He must have felt as if he were in enemy territory. Just like Willow would have been in, say, a bank. Or in a professional office that produces something

26

that couldn't be purchased in a struggling record store in which no one shops because the owner of the store doesn't have time for anybody who doesn't adore music the way he does, which is to say obsessively and unhealthily, not tethered in any way to the rational, *real* world.

"Top five songs to play when an asshole leaves a store," announces Skip loudly, in the grand hope that it drives out the remaining two customers. "Number five. Replacements, 'I Hate Music' …"

In the past, Skip has actually done much worse.

Once, he took a shotgun and fired at a customer who had the temerity to ask for a Marky Mark cassette for a sick daughter who most likely didn't exist.

The customer had died a gruesome death and his photo now hung over the cash register as a warning to anyone else foolish enough to have subpar taste.

Whatever. Corporate rock *still* sucks.

"He didn't seem … *too* bad," says Willow. "His eyes were … *kind*."

"*Whaaaaaaaat*?!" Skip exclaims. "Look at you! Growing *weak* in your old age!"

"Look who's talking! How old would that make *you*?" asks Willow.

"Twenty-nine," says Skip.

"Boomer," spits Willow.

"Hardly," hisses Skip. "Just an older Gen-Xer with *actual* taste."

"Skip, do you really not like The Beatles?"

"Prefer the Shaggs."

"Rolling Stones?"

"The Residents."

"Nirvana?"

"The Feelies."

"Maybe you're just too old," says Willow. "Definitely too old to *grunge*."

"Not old where it *counts*," says Skip, pointing to his crotch. "Here, aim your little camera down here and film this little monkey. There ya go. Bring in all those female viewers on the MTV."

Willow had forgotten all about the videocamera on her belt-loop.

What the hell is she doing inside a store, barely working, conversing with an oldster, when she could be outside in the real *world, beneath the miserable, authentic mist, creating her own future with people her own age, doing her own anti-thing?*

Besides, isn't working too hard not good for your health? And hadn't she once seen a bumper sticker on a broken-down Chevy van next to a clean-needle clinic that said as much?

"Real charmer," Willow says. "Anyway, gotta take a break. Don't scare off the *rest* of the customers."

"Don't you have the listening-station headphones to clean?" asks Skip.

He points over to where a teenager is listening to the latest release from the Dutch rap-rock band, Urban Dance Squad, but with the headphones pulled ever so slightly apart from his ears, so there is no actual contact. It's probably a smart move. The Great Seattle Lice Outbreak of '91 had originated from this very store. Patient X had been a sixteen-year-old fan of the

28

Soup Dragons who had forgotten his white bucket hat.

Mistake.

"Say hi to Vicky for me," says Skip.

"You should actually *speak* to her one day," says Willow. "It's fun to converse with a *real* human."

"Oh, I don't like to talk," says Skip. "I like to *think*. Also, to *make lists*."

"Still squishy for Vicky," says Willow. "You're an interesting guy. With a lot to say. But you just never *say* it. Only then will you have a *chance*."

"A chance?"

"Before you're too old."

"Twenty-nine and feelin' fine," says Skip, launching into a fresh list: "Top five songs to listen to when coming up with music lists and not making any human contact." Willow is no longer listening. "Number one: 'The Mayor of Simpleton' by XTC …"

Outside, Willow can't help but notice that not one of her friends has so much as moved. God bless 'em! She's so lucky to have found them!

Plus, this will only make the editing for continuity that much easier down the road …

The rain is lighter now but still creates an atmosphere conducive to some deep and philosophical talk.

"Ever take a shit that made you feel as if you were practically seven feet tall?" Jack Jack states. "Well, I'm feeling Charles Barkley large about now!"

"Just took a monstrous piss," declares Spooner. "I'm starting to get worry lines on my dick."

"Hey! It's Willow!" says Wes, from atop the roof. "You just missed a suburban poseur leaving!"

"Oh I saw him," she says.

"You notice what he was driving? A BMW! What a buckethead! Bet that moofer is *just* discovering *Nevermind*."

"And I thought *we* were the losers," said Spooner.

"We are. In a *good* way. *He's* the loser," says Cody, "you know, in a *bad* way."

It was confusing to most people but not to this group.

"At least we ain't the *phonies*," says Jack Jack.

"No, but we *are* the outliers," says Spooner. "We live on the outskirts of common decency and respectability!"

This was true … for instance, Cliph, a former member of the Lost Boys, was recently arrested and is now in jail for a scam involving Columbia House Records and Tapes.

One million records for one penny.

It made the international news.

The poor man is doing life.

But there's plenty to listen to …

"So tell me, Jack Jack," Willow asks. "I've heard a rumor."

"Really?"

"Yeah. That Brendan Bryant, the inventor of the greatest hacky sack in the world, is going to show, right here in this very parking lot. Do you think he actually will?"

"Why *wouldn't* he show? I mean, he *said* he would. Or his assistant said he would. We knew him when he was just a regular guy back in high school. What, you think he's too good now? Now that he's famous?"

Jack Jack rollerblades in a circle and then another. He pumps his fist like the innovative slacking winner he wills himself to be. One who'd rather hang out with cool friends in a parking lot than ever get started on some *bullshit* career.

"Right," agrees Wes. "Just because Brendan goes off to become the inventor of the most perfect hacky sack in the world doesn't mean he can't return to his parking lot roots."

"His hacky sack is rippin'!" says Code. "It's in the new colors of the South African flag! Saw it on a 2:00 A.M. infomercial! That's not subjugation. That's *respect*!"

"When I become famous," says Jack Jack, "I will *not* forget my roots."

"Famous for *what*?" asks Wes. "And what roots? *This*?"

"Famous for discovering that Evian spelled backwards is 'naïve.'"

"*Tihs On*," says Wes. "That's 'no shit' spelled backwards."

"It's hard to believe," says Cody, "it really is. Not about what you just said but that someone we all knew from this parking lot, someone we used to hang with, has gone off and become himself a multi-millionaire. Little Brendan Bryant. *Outrageous*."

"Dreams do come true, even in the Northwest," sarcasts Wes.

He sighs. Boeing is doing well, he supposes. There's been some talk about Microsoft in the news.

31

Other than that, the local economy is tanking. There's just nothing at all worthwhile that will ever come out of this area—might as well just keep crouching on a slanted roof …

"This city sucks a ginormous teat," says Jack Jack.

"Question," says Wes from the roof, impishly. "When you jack off, do you Jack Jack Off?"

"Hilarious," says Jack Jack. "But yes yes!" And then, in a soft voice, he asks: "Is it just me or do my palms smell funny?"

"Why not go home?" asks Wes. "To do more jack jackin'?"

"To my pup tent within a teepee beneath a canopy tent in my parent's garage?" says Jack Jack. "No thanks!"

Willow notices that Wake and Bake have arrived and are leaning against the record store's brick exterior. They are always together, *never* apart; both are from back East.

New Jersey, Willow thinks.

Bake talks, Wake doesn't. Or is it the other way around? Bake is fat and Wake is thin. Wake is wise and Bake dim. Or is it the other way around? *Wait.* Maybe they're *not* both from the East. How *do* they know each other again? Bake arrived before Nirvana A.D., but Wake didn't. Or *did* he?

Yes, Wake is the one who only communicates by tapping his forehead. One for yes. Twice for no.

Or is that Bake?

Doesn't matter … they are a *delight* to observe. Like a grungy Chang and Eng attached by their deep

32

love of selling illegal drugs cooked up in backyard shacks to pre-teens from broken families and who suffer from Attention Deficit Disorder.

Bake earns extra dough as a sign-twirler for a sushi restaurant. He's in charge of spinning the anthropomorphized salmonella bacteria. Wake likes to play Sega at his grandmother's. She has air conditioning. And free food.

And opioids.

Willow presses RECORD on her Fuji DS-100 digicam, the world's very first digital videocamera. A graduation present from her parents. Willow chose this gift over a brand-new car. She can scarcely believe the magic she is about to capture for all eternity. Her friends are *beyond* special!

"Let's talk about the Hulk. All green creatures have tremendous cocks. It's a proven cliché." It's Jack Jack.

"The Human Torch's lamb cannon can't even be measured. He'll just burn away the ruler with his blazing mutton musket!" It's Wes. /amb cannon

Now the rest join in: means genitals

"Let's talk about female superhero's tits. Wonder Woman! No competition. *Zero!*"

"But which version? Lynda Carter's? Or Susan Eisenberg's from the *Justice League* of the '70s?"

"Linda Carter! Her bibbly chunks are the bibbliest!"

"Baby bumpers!"

"Choozies!"

"Blubber baggos!"

"Darwin's dinglers!"

33

"God's gobblers!"

"*Flintstone's* Gazoos!"

Willow feels the chills sweep through her tiny body. It is all so much bigger and more important than she ever dreamed possible before she graduated from her fancy college on the east coast and had the opportunity to attend Yale Law but passed.

Sure, these friends of hers sometimes do and say silly things, but it'd be a shame not to capture them for all of eternity, right? Almost a crime against humanity!

Excitement throbs lazily within this soggy, veiny anarchist paradise. You can practically *feel* it way down in your *crunchers*.

Talk now turns to yet another fascinating topic: *Star Trek* and who is the most fuckable character: Uhuru from the original or Tasha Yar from *Next Generation?*

Bake says he'd love a blow job from one of them furry creatures, the Tribbles. He gets down on his knees and screams, "*Snoogums!*"

Wake says nothing but he gives a slow-motion nod in an alternative fashion: steady, sure, consistent. It is like something you'd see performed by an MTV VeeJay on "120 Minutes" just before he introduces a music video of strenuously-scruffy musicians in an empty warehouse, huge fan twirling lazily in the background for no perceptible reason, candelabras lit with candles purchased in bulk, poetic dust motes spinning aimlessly within the gorgeously mote-flecked light.

Is Wake brain damaged from too many bong hits?

Or is he just very stupid? Or is he so smart that no one can figure him out?

Is all of this parking lot reality merely just a figment of Bake's imagination?

These are questions for the ages.

Or at least for the early '90s.

Regardless, Wake says nothing.

Jack Jack adjusts his hillbilly hat and smirks. He sucks on a rubber baby blinky attached by string to a leather necklace.

Minutes ago, he sold his Jamaican Tam to a white kid for a bag of BBQ Cheetos.

Topper skateboards past. Up on the slanted roof, Wes remains seated at an awkward angle.

Topper says, "My life is a Truffaut film, baby."

"Have you ever actually seen Truffaut, baby?" asks Bake, from against the wall.

"Not yet, baby," says Topper. "Soon, baby. Baby, *soon!*"

One thousand miles from this location sits the gravestone of the great Charles Bukowski, the spiritual leader of all grungers. The inscription on the grave simply reads "Don't Try."

Willow is thinking of getting the phrase tattooed on her forearm.

The *perfect* philosophy for anyone to live by.

Suddenly, without warning, Skip rushes out of the record store, aiming a rifle at a fleeing customer holding a *Best of Journey* compact disc, paid for with a credit card.

The gang laughs.

rockville pike to falls rd. to bell mill to gainsborough, 10321. 8pm Saturday

That Skip sure hates his mainstream rock!

Meanwhile, in the background, a thumping song can be heard … loud and strong.

It's called "N.Y.A. (Not. Yet. Adults.)"

Willow has heard this particular song a million times already. But she sings along, regardless.

She adores it.

And before long, all the Lost Boys are joining in:

Yeah, that was me at the poetry slam,
Takin' a leak on my ex-girlfriend's van.
Just another night in this fucked-up life
Because I'm N.Y.A and it cuts like a knife!

They call us loafers and layabouts.
Slackers, slouchers, shirkers,
surfers of that there couch.
The system so rigged! The system so fake!
Not yet an adult, just wanna get baked!

Mom and dad, they hate me, they say I'm a waste,
Not those words exactly, but I know I'm a disgrace.
"Can you take a shower for our Thanksgiving dinner?"
Just 'cause I got dreads, make me some kinda sinner?!

I get the same shit treatment when I go to the mall:

The arcade, Orange Julius, JC Penny's Big and Tall.
Even at the record store I'm taking tons of heat.
Just because I shoplift, they kick me to the street!

They call us loafers and layabouts.
Slackers, slouchers, shirkers, surfers of that there couch.

The system so rigged! The system so fake!
Not yet an adult, just wanna get baked!

Last night, stayed up till dawn finishing my new zine,
Writin' 'bout those sell-outs on the whole Seattle scene.
The stuffed shirt at the Kinkos goes and charges me 12 bucks!
I left it all just sitting there, said I don't give 12 fucks!
That's the night I got real high and went to 7-Eleven.

My bros and I stayed there so long, the cops, they started meddlin',
I yelled for revolution, said we won't take this no more!
My folks bailed me out, then grounded me with chores.

Guess you're a baby boomer,
And I'm Gen X.
I mostly hate the hippies,
But I dig their views on sex!
I stand for everything, I stand for nothing, too.
Life, it moves so fast!
You've gotta make the moment last.

That's okay, I get it, you don't like this here
view.
So suck it ... times twenty-two.

Prof. Doherty fell asleep during class today

Wednesday, 1:35 P.M.

"Let's take it from the top," announces Toody, stroking his soul patch. It is in the shape of a perfectly-formed question mark—Toody thinks it signifies his philosophy pretty damn well.

He might as well look good while barely existing, right?

As if to prove this point, Toody is wearing his special black spandex cycling shorts over his white cotton long-underwear that's been jaggedly cut off just beneath the knees.

Combined with the flannel work shirt he's found at a garage sale, he looks supremely casual. The shirt was sold by the widow of the man who wore it for twenty-five years before dying of a heart attack at the gas station where he toiled for less than minimum wage.

It's a cool look, months before Urban Outfitters will adopt anything even remotely similar for five times the price.

In his right nostril, Toody has inserted one foam ear plug. No one dares question why. *Spin* magazine had already written about Toody's special look, calling it "thrift shop hip."

The Tower Records in-house magazine, *Pulse!*, had disagreed, calling it a look you might see inside a hospital for the "insane," but Toody takes this as a compliment.

He might as well look insane while barely exist-

ing, right?

Being crazy is a *cool* thing.

Genius or insane person?

Both?

Don't much matter ...

Regardless, it's so much cooler to be insane than to be a "cob nobbler," a term Toody just read about in an article in the *New York Times* about grunge. He intends to adopt this word, as well as all the others—maybe even claim that he was the one who coined them. "Cob nobbler" means "loser."

But not a good loser. *hard for us to understand*

A bad loser. *but they understood*

A loser who doesn't want to be a loser.

It gets complicated. But every Gen X'er *knows*.

Toody grew up three hours west of Seattle, in Aberdeen. He knew the Great Man, himself. Didn't know him all *too* well—Kurt was a little quiet and selfish and a bit into himself—but Toody sat next to him in home room and watched him closely. Also not the chatty type. Head in his journal. Bit of a loner, truth be told.

Mopey.

Toody would sometimes tease him between classes.

But Toody studied Kurt. And when the time was right, Toody emerged like a loose-fitting, unkempt butterfly from out of his lethargic chrysalis, straight into the narcotic '90s.

Toody now has *reason*.

While others zig, he *zags*.

Now is his time to *drably* shine.

Toody has attempted to reach out to Kurt. To thank him for being such an influence. He's yet to hear back. But it's just a matter of time. Because once Kurt learns that these two are now creative equals, he'll surely be in touch, perhaps even eager to take part in Willow's MTV documentary.

Toody is sure of it.

They practically came up together!

"Hey, Wills," says Toody to Willow. "What's the *tribulation*?"

Toody bats his large, brown eyes. It's one of his best features not hidden by clothing. There is a definite sex appeal to Toody … not hurt by the copious amount of gas-station sexual-enhancement pills he consumes daily.

"I've *missed* you!" says Willow, meaning it. "Have you missed *me*? I haven't seen you in a few days!"

"Did you like my fax! The one I sent this morning?" Toody asks.

"Of your penis?" explains Willow.

"Could you feel my *urgency?*" asks Toody. "Might be worth something if you keep it long enough. I used the fax machine at the library."

"It's … *lovely*," says Willow.

"*Whaaaaaat*?" asks Toody. "I didn't *hear* you."

Toody has a touch of tinnitus, the "club disease."

"*Lovely*!" says Willow louder. "Your faxed penis was *lovely*!"

"I *get* it," half-screams Toody, not getting it.

"Anyway, I missed you Toods. Was thinking we

41

could get together tonight at the Bean There and play some board games."

"Board games? Willow, are we going out or something? Going steady?"

"I … thought we were," says Willow. "Aren't we?"

"*You're spizzin' off the spazz wazz!* You know I'm slammin' on other Bettys!"

"Aw, c'mon," says Willow. "I *know* you love me, Toods! And you're trying to play it real cool but …"

What in the hell is she talking about? Toody stares at Willow's mouth as it moves. It's hypnotic.

It keeps moving. Toody hears nothing.

"From the top," Toody eventually declares, blinking himself out of his spell.

He grabs a super-fuzz distortion box which he carries around and speaks into whenever he wants to sound extra alternative, which is practically all the time.

Like now:

"From the top!" he declares, this time through the box.

Willow steps away. Maybe he's just in his "creative zone." She'll talk to him later. Or not.

What she *won't* be doing is crowding him.

True artists are like cats. If you get too close, they're liable to panic, shit, and vomit. In rare cases, cause terrible injury to vulnerable body parts. Best to just keep your distance until they need something.

Toody's band is called That's Your Problem and it is now swinging on the "flippity-flop."

The previous band's name was Jim's Flavor-Aid.

42

They are loud. Crushing. Extreme. And they have only six days to practice before MTV arrives to choose one band from the entire Seattle area—and only one from the thousands—to be launched into super stardom in the wake of Nirvana's colossal success.

"The Great MTV Grunge Off"!

First year in existence. Live. On the air. The entire world tuning in!

That's Your Problem is expected to win.

Not one member of the band plays an instrument.

Doesn't matter.

It's all about the look ... it's all about the collective alienation ...

Up on the makeshift stage, Toody takes a flying leap into the audience—or an audience if there happened to be an audience.

There is only a tumbling mat.

"That was extreme, dude," says Tad, the bass player, not the drummer who is also named Tad.

Toody nods.

Yeah. It was. It was truly very good.

Toody is a twenty-four-year old who feels there is so much more to life than working five hours a week as a bike messenger delivering hand-blown glass crackpipes to bow-tied lunchers in the business district: specifically, his face on the cover of *Spin* magazine, frowning, scrunching his shoulders to show just how painful it feels to have the weight of the entire world resting on them.

He plans to wear a "Corporate Magazines STILL Suck" T-shirt and brag that he'll soon be dating top

43

junkie models.

Toody has an air of danger and a sensuality reminiscent of an aged Jim Morrison.

Once, back in Aberdeen, he failed a mirror self-recognition test typically used on monkeys and other higher functioning mammals. He punched at the mirror and howled in frustration. He thinks of himself as the *chosen one*.

If nothing else, Toody is the first man in his family to have ever worn belted jeans without a shirt.

He's a kind man, who loves nothing more than to visit sick children in the hospital.

One day he'll ask permission first.

Beyond these noble achievements, Toody is also the inventor of the "crouch sing," squatting awkwardly, one foot stretched towards the crowd, one foot propping up his ass, two hands grabbing the microphone. He's copyrighted this move on a bar napkin … but never had it registered. A genius with ideas, but not the best with follow through.

Toody is every character in an S.E. Hinton novel who allows his younger brothers to eat pizza for breakfast and pancakes for dinner.

Willow is his biggest fan.

True, he never apologizes after farting … but you can't have it all.

"That was amazing!" exclaims Willow. There is a rawness to Toody that is missing in Willow's own genetic makeup. Although she was a straight-A English major back at her fancy Northeast college— of which she received a full ride courtesy of a poetry-slam scholarship—she'd so much rather be a seamstress for the grunge band, not that they would ever particularly need one.

"Yeah," says Toody, through the super-fuzz distortion box. "*Anguish*! Angst, you know?"

Toody find it easier to communicate his feelings by simply announcing them rather than going through the laborious process of having others attempt to decipher them.

"We going out tonight?" asks Willow. "Been looking forward to it all day. Yesterday was a tough one at work. Three customers! I'm exhausted!"

"No," says Toody, still speaking through his box. "Have to practice my guitar-solo prance. Like, when the guitarist does his solos, or would if he could play and I have nothing else to do but to just stand there. Like *then*."

Willow understands.

"Maybe another time," she says.

"Maybe," says Toody. His attention dissipates like a simile of something or other. "Then again, maybe not. *Tormentttt*!"

His heroin-induced insouciance is delicious. Willow wouldn't trade it for the world!

"Okay. Well, see ya," says Willow, as casual as she can muster but not quite as casually as she was hoping for. This is not easy for her. She doesn't have the *knack*.

"Cool Ranch," says Toody, climbing back onstage with a little help from Tad the guitarist. "I'm starting at five feet. Then gonna work my way up—hoping to leap from a *fifteen* foot speaker stack by the time MTV arrives!"

Willow doesn't doubt Toody. When he puts his mind to something, he is unstoppable. Like that rock fest he organized in '88 to shed light on women in the mosh pit. From the stage, as three women were being terribly injured, he had announced it was "time to allow the feminine species to reign *everywhere*, even in that most male of arenas: *the mosh pit*. Open up the pits to girls! I love them girls' pits!"

Jim Gordon in *Rolling Stone* had deemed it a great, historical move forward for women. Three women died for the cause, which made it all that much more significant.

"Okay, well, talk to you soon," says Willow.

Toody says nothing.

Willow walks out of the practice space and back into her own apartment. There are twelve large apartments in this four-story building on Capitol Hill.

Willow is friends with every Gen X'er within them. This is the way it works in Seattle in the early 1990s. *No doors.* If a friend wants to chat, they just walk into the next apartment and do so. *A den of slack.* No doors. I just said that.

In the front of the building, within the courtyard, a fountain burbles soothingly. The rent is $495 a month, way too much for a simple MTV documentarian with a 12-hour-a-week record-store job.

But not too much for her parents back east to pay due to the relative safety of this building's location and the fountain out front that burbles so soothingly.

46

Better, each apartment contains huge wood spools and at least one very modern, tremendously large halogen lamp.

Vicky—Willow's roommate for two weeks now (ever since they met on the plane that landed in Seattle)—is already eating breakfast in the apartment's nook, just next to the split-bamboo rolled blinds and the milk crate that holds philosophy books stolen from the library.

The two immediately bonded over their love of the Northwest and their hatred of their hometowns back East.

The Northwest is their *future*.

The Northeast was their *past*.

Vicky is into swing dancing and plastic hair barrettes.

Vicky is into bands who combine gypsy jazz, Delta blues, Klezmer, Theremin horror and anything involving medieval instruments.

Vicky only cooks "light" but can't lose the weight she gained in the 1980s from all those fat-free Dove bars.

Vicky draws fliers for alternative bands and staples them to telephone poles. In most cases, she's sleeping with the lead singer.

Vicky never wakes before noon.

Vicky imbibes boysenberry wine.

Vicky writes and edits her own hand-lettered Fanzine—or "zine"—about the author Naomi Wolfe and third-wave feminism. It has a circulation of ten. She is never without her X-Acto knife, glue stick, and

47

box of crayons. The zine is called "The Wolfe Pact."

Vicky adores men.

All men.

But especially those who are sweaty and unceremonious in their tight black chokers. That's the way she *likes* 'em: sludgier and grungier. And they like her right on back, at least for the night.

"Want to meet up later for a drink?" Vicky asks, nibbling on a microwavable stack of "light" waffles. "Maybe rent a party beer ball?" Her Romanian clove cigarette dangles from her mouth. "After work? You could probably use one or five."

Vicky stubs out the ash next to the syrup.

"Would *love* to, Vips, but I need to capture the brilliance of my generation."

Vicky nods. She understands. "Guess I'll just keep getting high off of life, is all."

"Besides, we're waiting for Brendan Bryant to show up in the lot."

"The inventor of the hacky sack with the new South African colors? From the infomercial? *Please!* I'll believe *that* when I see it!"

"This could *really* happen. He'll be in town. I give the odds at 50%," says Willow. "Want to meet him? I'll call from the pay phone. Or page your beeper?"

"I'm booked *super* solid," says Vicky. "I have my, like, swing-dancing lessons. And then over to the cigar bar to meet Rod. We're gonna talk about what we can do to help the environment."

On the wall, behind the television, is a spray-painted message that read:

48

We shall not EXXONerate!

Next to that one is another spray-painted message, this in MTV font:

bombSHELL

Beneath that sign is the word "ESSO." The word is bookended by other letters so that it spells out:

oprESSOrs

Handsprayed graffiti slogans make an exceedingly serious environmental point. This is definitely *serious* business!

But Vicky and Willow have run out of large oil companies to disparage, at least with the names of companies that can be used effectively within other words.

Plus, they imagine that their boomer landlord might not be as socially conscious as they are, which is a shame and a bit sad.

"Wait," says Willow, picking up her sheepskin-lined denim jacket draped haphazardly across the well-worn couch. "Who's Rod?"

"The lutist from Bean There coffee shop," says Vicky, taking another cloved drag.

"Weren't you sleeping with *another* lutist?" Willow asks, perplexed. "Who worked at a bookstore that only sold communist manifestos?"

There is only one coffee house in Seattle where everyone of a certain age likes to "hang." Happily for Vicky, it features local musicians who play medieval instruments. Also board games, such as Life and Candyland.

And serves breakfast cereal and Fluffernutter sandwiches. *marshmellow food*

And for those who like to eat as if they're once again a helpless, shit-flicking toddler, strained vegetables and pureed fruits on baby-friendly, divided plates.

"That would be Jethro," says Vicky. "But he doesn't play the lute anymore. He plays the hurdy-gurdy. Wait. No, that was *Ebeneezer*."

"Super *alterna*," says Willow, mentally tabulating the amount of men Vicky has slept with in just the past week. She counts up to ten and stops. The thing about Vicky is that she's attractive, most certainly, but not in the traditional, cinematic sense. Perhaps that's why she tends to sleep around more. Or perhaps it has more to do with Vicky constantly announcing in public—even once in line at the Motor Vehicles Administration—that she is very much "in touch with her sexuality."

Vicky used to have a lame job as a caretaker at a hospice tending to the dying. But it was a McJob run by a strict boss who just didn't understand Vicky's need to "have fun."

She had worked there for an hour before being fired for dancing in her socks to "Girls Just Want to Have Fun."

Behind the kitchen table—linoleum and chrome,

retro—is a radio. Vicky flicks on the power. It's time for "Tellin' It Like It Is," Seattle's daily pirate radio broadcast on 10-watt FM mono station 88.3.

The voice is that of DJ Morning Glory—aka, DJ Truth—the coolest DJ in all Seattle. All Gen X'ers listen each and every morning:

"We're all in this together. I believe in the human spirit. I believe in love. I'm in love with love. Won't someone be in love with me? I would love that. And I think you would love that I'd love that also ..."

No one knows for certain who the real man is behind this bold, plummy, masculine voice, but the entire city knows what this man *represents*.

Seattle *before* the hordes arrive.

Willow and Vicky are grandfathered in. They landed two weeks ago, a few minutes before MTV premiered "Smells Like Teen Spirit" and a few hours after the soap opera *General Hospital* played a Mudhoney song during a colonoscopy scene ("In 'n' Out of Grace").

Willow sometimes laughs at how innocent she was then: not wearing a stitch of black, and stinking of Country Apple Body Splash bought at a store appealing to the happy.

"He just needs someone to love," echoes Vicky.

"Sure sounds like it," says Willow.

"There's too much darkness and not enough light. Let's all let in the light! Let the light come

shining through! Let's do this together, me and you...." speaks wiseness. Deux machina

"God, I wish I could meet someone this smooth-talking in real life," says Vicky. "I'm so tired of dating men who don't talk. Or who just grunt their affections."

"One day you might," says Willow, doubting it. "I'll see you tonight. If you have a ... very *special* guest, place a hair band around your bedroom's door-knob."

"Say hi to Skip," says Vicky and laughs. "Poor guy has zero game!"

"Will do. Maybe tomorrow we go *thrifting*?"

"Sounds *score*," says Vicky, using the latest in grunge slang. "Sounds *real score*."

Willow exits the apartment, clutching an ironic *Charlie's Angels* lunchbox that contains her lunch (a PB and J with the crust cut off).

If Willow is lucky, she'll arrive to work to find Toby the Wonder Pooch dressed as one of the Angels. Or even Charlie, himself!

Willow needs something—*anything*—to take her mind off the three hours of pseudo-work that exists before her.

She takes the freight elevator down and into the courtyard and past the fountain, then over to her recumbent bicycle with the safety flag (featuring a pirate skull and crossbones) locked against a wrought-iron fence. She attaches her Fuji DS-100 digicam with 3-power zoom to the handlebars with a bungee-chord, facing outward, and presses RECORD.

Can't afford to lose even one potential shot!

What she is doing is *that* important.

Not just for her.

For humankind.

The streets are slick, cinematically so, the puddles reflecting back the local attractions: the modernity of the Space Needle, the splendor of Mt. Rainier, the Pike Place Market, where fish is tossed for the amusement of easily-amused locals and foreign tourists wearing pleated jeans.

Seated in her recumbent bicycle, cruising through the city streets on her way to work, earphones attached to her banana-yellow Sony SPORTS Walkman (waterproof, shock proof), Willow thinks back on her college graduation ceremony. She graduated summa cum laude from a school with the Latin motto: *Tanto maiore pecunia artium historiam modo consumptis.*

Translated loosely it comes out as: "One spends way too much money on an art history major."

She had been chosen as the student speaker.

Wearing flip-flops beneath her graduation robe, and with *Pomp and Circumstance in D Minor* warbling over the sound system, Willow had confidently stepped up to the lectern and looked out across the huge crowd.

She pointed to her parents, sitting just a few rows back:

"I want to thank you—and that's *you*, mom and dad—for what you've provided for me. It hasn't been easy but I've *made it*!"

She waited for the applause that was sure to arrive. After it did, she continued confidently:

"I also want to thank you for showing me what *not* to do. And who *not* to become …"

There were murmurs amongst those in the audience, especially those above the age of twenty-five.

Willow ignored them.

Fuck do they know?

"In your comfortable—"

She practically spit out the word "comfortable"—

"… suburban houses, with your wasteful lawns and your plastic fences to keep out all those *scary* urban invaders. With your blue BMWs and easy-listening Muzak. With your colorful clothing and easy answers. Like lambs to the slaughter, marching together lock-step straight out of your pens and into the killing fields, without a sound, without so much as one *solitary* complaint. *Pathetic*! *Ponderous*! But I will *not* do that!"

There was some applause, scattered among the older parents and relatives. *Screw them all.* They didn't understand that today was a *new dawn.* Consumerism was dead. There is no reason for *anything*.

Slouchin' toward Slackerdem.

Doin' nothin' and nothin' doin' …

Encouraged by the positive reception, Willow had continued: "You can take your eighty-hour work weeks and *stuff* them! You can take your Nike shoes and run circles with them! You can take your German contraptions and drive off a damn cliff with them! It is time for a fresh generation to do what the Boomers

54

couldn't! It's time to clean up this mess they left us! *Fellow graduates …*"

Willow paused. There was only one thing left say:

"BURN THE WORLD DOWN WITH LETHARGY!" she cried.

Willow had once read this phrase in the *Anarchist Cookbook* she had stolen from a B. Dalton's. Now was the *perfect* time to plagiarize it.

Now *that's* anarchy!

Throwing her cap into the air—in direct solidarity with those suffering in East Africa, or was it *South Africa?*—Willow gave the victory sign and pointed offstage.

The song "My Sharona" by the Knack kicked in over the sound system, loud and crunching. The thirtysomethings and olders winced. ~song popular back then~

Not Willow. ~they'd dance to it in public places~

Willow danced on stage as some of her braver friends joined her in unity, crazily and uninhibitedly. They boogied and swayed until the graduation speaker—*a Desmond Tata? Tonto?, Willow had never heard of the guy, he wasn't young and he wasn't handsome*—complained until Willow and the rest were dragged off by security.

Guy just wasn't into the "kook."

The nerve. *Fuck 'em all. And fuck her parents!*

She'd never have to talk to them again! Time for a new and purposeless life in a moister location—

Willow is thrown backwards, out of her recumbent bicycle and onto the street. The force is awesome.

She finds herself staring at a gray sky. *What just*

55

happened? The sound of South African township music can be heard. Is she hallucinating? A white singer warbling over African backup singers. Is Willow back at graduation? Has everything that's happened since been a mere hallucination?

Or is she in soggy heaven?

Is musical subjugation a thing there, too?

"Record store girl?"

Willow squints upwards.

It's Mr. Straight, blocking out the sun, or the sun that would exist if Seattle ever saw it.

The music blasting out from the car is *Graceland* by Paul Simon, *the* album Willow considers to be representative of the worst that North American singers in particular, and the Western Hemisphere in general, have to offer.

Her parents listen to it nonstop.

Colonialists.

"My god! I'm so sorry! I had a map out, not paying attention!" says Mr. Straight earnestly. He's practically screaming. "I drive this route every morning but I had a map blocking my view this time! Last time it was the airbag and this time it was the map."

"On my way to work," mumbles Willow. "*Must* get to work to not work …"

"Here, let me help you stand," says Mr. Straight.

Willow notices his car is a BMW. Just as Wes had told her. With CALIFORNIA license plates. *Double figures.*

And, as Wes had said, there are no bumper stickers. Not one about ACT UP or the AIDS COALI-

TION TO UNLEASH POWER and not a thing about animal rights.

Who has no bumper stickers? Only those with zero concerns about the world's complexities, that's who …

"I'm afraid you won't be going anywhere with this bike," says Mr. Straight, pointing to the back tire, bent, deflated. "Were you asleep? You were lying back."

"Recumbent," mumbles Willow, standing—or trying to. Feels like a twisted ankle. She takes a step forward but falls back, caught just in time by Mr. Straight. It doesn't look as if she'll be headed to work this morning to hardly accomplish anything, after all. There goes $15 for her three hours of toil.

"Let me put this in the trunk," Mr. Straight says, picking up the bike as if it weighs nothing and placing it within his red BMW. *He hasn't even asked permission!* "Let's get you to a hospital right quick."

Willow is gently led over to the car. Before entering, she takes a glance inside for anything that might signify that this man could be a danger to her and best be avoided—say, a knife, or a rope, or a T-shirt that reads I AM THE GREEN RIVER KILLER.

No. Just a huge and floppy zippered-canvas CD binder with hundreds of vinyl sleeves and one issue of *Vanity Fair* with a hefty, dowdy woman on the cover.

Willow doesn't know who this woman is. An overweight actress? A very bloated singer from the vaudeville era?

Mrs. Doubtfire?

Willow looks closer. No. Just the new president

of the United States, Bill Clinton.

"Hospital's only ten minutes away," Mr. Straight says, helping her into the car and running around to the driver's side. "I can get you there in no time at all! I'll put the map down!"

He seems most excited by this adventure.

Willow has to admit that it feels good for a man to be paying attention to her. It's been awhile. The last time Toody had acted all the gentleman had been when he had paid extra for those tighter, higher-end condoms and not the baggier, "loose-fit" distressed variety he typically purchased at the dollar store with pocket change.

"Don't really think that's necessary," says Willow. "Just a bruise. Will be fine. But I *do* need to call my boss. Can we stop somewhere to call?"

"That won't be necessary," says Mr. Straight, pulling out from the glove compartment—*and Willow can't believe this, could it even be possible?*—a cellular car phone!

Willow had thought only presidents and balding action stars owned cellular car phones!

"No need," says Mr. Straight, as if reading her mind. "Just call with *this*. I use it all the time. For my work."

"What do you do?"

"Business."

"*Business?*"

"Yes."

This guy was *important*.

"What specifically about Business?"

58

"Just ... *Business*," he says, handing over the phone. "Finance. Business. *Commerce*. Before that, I was involved with environmental matters."

"My roommate and I absolutely *love* the environment!" says Willow. "What did you do? Hijack and dynamite whale-fishing boats?"

"No, no! A little of *this*. A little of *that*."

"But what exactly?" asks Willow. "About the environment?" *when ppl started loving the enviroment*

Mr. Straight shrugs.

Maybe he's just being modest.

Willow rolls down her window and sticks the six-inch antenna out. It's expandable. It reminds her of a dog's penis. She dials the store's number. It goes through.

This is a technological miracle.

This is like calling from the moon!

"Yeah?" says Skip, in a foul mood even when answering the phone.

"Bet you'll never guess where *I'm* calling from," Willow says, unable to move because of the coiled cord hooked beneath the pleathered handbrake.

"The rubber room?"

"Very funny. From *a car*. That's moving."

"You sell out?"

"*Never*," says Willow.

"You coming in today?"

"Don't think so. Actually ... I just got into an *accident*." Willow pauses. She whispers: "You'll never guess with who."

"The idiot who was in the store buying Aero-

59

smith?" Skip asks.

"Yeah ... how did you know?"

"Just a seventh sense."

"What was he listening to when he hit you?"

"*Graceland.* Paul Simon."

"Pathetic. You know what would have been better? 'Girlfriend in a Coma' by the Smiths. *Hmmm.* What would be number two? Depeche Mode, 'Enjoy the Silence'?"

"See you tomorrow," says Willow.

She goes to hang up but can't quite figure out how. Before she manages to find the OFF button, Willow can hear Skip hurling abuse at a customer who has dared to ask for a *Best of Kansas* CD.

"Dust in my fucking asshole, you ... *asshole*!"

"What a peach!" says Mr. Straight, when Willow hangs up. He's overheard the conversation. "Terrific boss you work for there. A real *gem*!"

Willow laughs. "He's just a guy who ... I don't know, likes people with good taste."

"Taste that totally mimics his?"

"I guess."

"So are you saying I don't have any?" asks Mr. Straight, turning up *Graceland*. He doesn't appear disheartened, only mildly curious.

"I'm saying ..." begins Willow, but stops. "I don't know. Who knows?"

She turns down *Graceland*. It's only making her sensibility throb.

She ain't no "NPR Nancy."

"I suggest that we have breakfast," says Mr.

Straight. "It's the *least* I can do."

Is he asking her out on a date? If so, what exactly would be the harm? She has nothing to do for the rest of the day besides work. And who wants that? Life languidly stretches before her into an empty infinity. All she has is time ...

"I would rather see your workplace," says Willow, staring out the window.

It comes across more boldly than she had intended but she likes the sound of it.

"Would you now?" Mr. Straight asks, with a slight grin.

Willow has seen a million comedies in which a man and a woman meet in a cute fashion, such as in that film in which the rich woman is out walking her dog on a New York City street through gorgeous snowdrifts but then trips and falls over a homeless man who is urinating a heart with an arrow through it and they then instantly fall in love.

Or in that other film about a man smuggling 80 wax-coated balls of hashish in his stomach on that overnight flight from Turkey. He meets a young, gorgeous customs officer at O'Hare who has been put in charge of making sure the laxatives forced down his throat do their job.

It is all very romantic.

But in real life, Willow has never once heard of a woman falling in love after being hit on a recumbent bike by a man in a BMW without a single socially-conscious bumper sticker.

Then again, this doesn't mean that this relationship

couldn't work. At the very least, she'd get to spend an innocent day at a professional office, with real syndicated comic-strips taped inside cubicles, with actual work being done for a very tangible reason.

She's always meant to see such a thing.

"Yes," she says. "I would. Really. But I have to be honest with you."

"Always," says Mr. Straight.

"I gave my graduation speech on capitalism and commerce," Willow announces and waits for his reaction.

His reaction is laughter.

"What's so funny?"

"For or against?"

"Against."

"I'd love to hear it one day."

"Play your cards right and maybe you will."

Willow can't believe what she just said. *Such boldness!* But why not? She's in the *real world* now. With *real-life* adventures! *Anything* can happen!

The ride to the office takes only a few minutes, but it's enough for Willow to learn that Mr. Straight's real name is Kevin Franklin—Kev to his friends and colleagues—and that he's been in the city for less than one year, originally from Sacramento, isn't yet married, has never heard of the underground writer Lester Bangs, has never seen the *Star Wars* holiday special, is twenty-six years old, a man with no greater aspiration than to work very hard at an important job inside a well-lit office, have a few wonderful children, and to live a good, decent life. He attended

[handwritten margin note: flirting here like a couple in 1930s rom-com]

62

Lallopalooza the previous year—the first year of its existence—but left early when a "grunge mime" took center stage and spent an hour walking through a driving rain without complaint.

When they reach Kevin's office, in downtown Seattle, Willow sees that there are many professional chairs, as well as sizeable computers and even a few typewriters and a water cooler or two. There's a "Fun Hang Area" filled with foosball and pool tables. There's a large chainsaw-carved wood sign that reads, in block letters, "Your Business Is My Business Consulting."

There's even a wood underline beneath "My."

When Willow asks one of Chip's cubicled co-workers what exactly she does in this professional office, day after day, week after week, year after year, the woman—in blazer and white stockings—answers, "Commerce," and Willow nods knowingly. There is an office kitchen and an office meeting space and an empty box of donuts because it is Wednesday and she has been told that the office always has donuts on Wednesdays. There are pens and paper and erasers. Heaps of Xerox paper. Envelopes. A few people working hard. The rest daydreaming about piercing hidden body parts.

She learns more about Kevin: he owns three CDs—*Graceland*, the soundtrack to the musical *Cats*; and his latest acquisition, *Best of Aerosmith*. In Sacramento, he had dated a fellow USC grad named Kerry for two years before she up and moved to Philadelphia to work for Teach for America.

She had broken up with him via registered mail.

Sorry, she had written, *I met a snowboarder named Max. He once modeled for* Sassy.

Willow passes a cubicle with a sign that reads in fancy, cursive dot-matrix: BEAM ME UP, SCOTTY!

If Willow didn't know it before she arrived here, she *definitely* knows it now: this place is *important*.

"This is Ben," says Mr. Straight, as a young co-worker approaches. "He's in charge of trust exercises for the office."

"Hi," says Ben.

"Hi," says Willow. "What are trust exercises? Like you fall into another's arms? Or you blindfold a person and have them navigate a room?"

Ben laughs. "No, that was the '80s."

"What's the exercise now?"

"Trusting that the <u>company won't look into your personal information on your</u> computer."

"That's terrible," says Willow. "Who would you ever do that?"

companies did this then

Ben remains silent. *and* **STILL** *do*

Mr. Straight laughs nervously and pushes Willow along.

"And this is Marcy!" Mr. Straight says, a bit too eagerly. "She's in charge of Donut Wednesdays!"

Marcy is too busy to talk. She scuttles past like an animated lobster. Willow wonders if all Wednesdays are this busy for her.

"Would you like a donut?" asks Mr. Straight. "Or watery coffee in a paper cup in jazzy purple and turquoise design?"

(STEWART)

She nods her head no.

Willow passes a sad-looking man wearing a Baltimore Orioles hat playing computer solitaire. His name is Mike and he's generally left alone.

So this is what an office is like! thinks Willow. Growing up, she's only worked as a babysitter for a few dollars. She spent the rest of her free time writing poetry about the unbearable loneliness Emily Dickinson must have felt not being invited to prom.

Emily Dickinson: the original grunger!

Willow passes a Green Peace bumper sticker attached to a cubicle's wall.

Warrior, thinks Willow. *This heroic woman in front of her large computer with the milky-green screen and blinking white cursor is yet another combatant for our beautiful goddess, Earth!*

This is all so fascinating, Willow thinks. *I could really get into this!*

"Hello, Kevin," says a passing male co-worker, drinking from a huge ceramic mug of coffee.

"Hi, Kev," says another passing co-worker, this one female, but also drinking from a huge ceramic mug of coffee.

"C'mon, Willow," Kevin says. "I want to show you my office. Do you like lucite?"

Mr. Straight works in a glass-enclosed office that sits dramatically in the center of it all. And a map of Seattle with giant X's marked all over.

"What are those X's?" asks Willow, pointing.

"Locations," says Mr. Straight, taking a seat in an Aeron chair. Willow recognizes it as the same type her father uses at his law firm. "Of our businesses."

"Can I look?" asks Willow.

"Sure," says Mr. Straight, feet up on his lucite desk, arms behind his head.

"So many," says Willow. She looks closer. "And even some near the record store."

"We might just bump into each other again soon."

"Ha," says Willow.

"You sure you don't want a donut?" Mr. Straight asks.

"No, I'm good," says Willow, looking around. It's all so neat compared to Skip's office! *And no funny rubber chickens! And not a single "NO DUMPING!" sign to be seen!*

Willow picks up a round lucite paperweight. She reads it: "'I'll take care of it when I get *round* to it.'"

"And it's *round*," says Mr. Straight, smiling. "It's *funny*."

"It is," says Willow. She walks over to a small device that holds five metal balls hanging from wires.

"That's an Executive Ball Clicker," says Mr. Straight. "Pull back the first ball."

Willow pulls the far right ball to the side and lets it go. The balls swing back and forth, colliding, clicking to the right, then to the left, then to the right. She watches the movements, the steady and sooth-ing clickety-clicks of its officious rhythmic clicki-ty-*swack*, clickity-*swack*.

Yes, Willow thinks, *this is even more romantic than the guy shitting out the smuggled 80 wax-coated balls of hashish!*

This *really* could work!

Later that afternoon, after Mr. Straight drops Willow off at her apartment building and drives back to his lame suburban home, after Willow notices a hair band tied around Vicky's doorknob, after Willow places an ice pack on her ankle, after she watches MTV's *120 Minutes*, after she tries to fall asleep—not so easy considering the noises of pleasure emanating from Vicky's bedroom, which, to Willow, sound a lot more like the screams in the final scene of *Amadeus*, within the madhouse—Willow does eventually fall asleep, and—for the first time in a week—fails to have a dream about Toody ignoring her while he half-heartedly designs his band's cassette demo, the tape that contains no music, just random sounds of fans applauding his most exceptional, nearly flawless stage dive from a stage monitor.

Mr. Straight had not asked her out for a date— either when he dropped her off or since by phone— but that's fine.

Willow has a feeling that she will see him again soon. Everyone runs into *everyone* in Seattle, typically while being filmed while pretending they're not.

A song can be heard from Willow's small radio. She turns it up. And sings along.

It's called "Lazy in Love":

> *Lazy 'bout work, lazy 'bout school,*
> *Lazy 'bout dope crunks,*
> *Can't bother to be cool.*
> *Ain't no thang, baby:*

Let's be lazy in love.

Lazy 'bout my folks, lazy 'bout my friends,
Lazy 'bout them bills, all that money I get lent.
It's all good, baby: let's be lazy in love.

I know you want that diamond ring,
Or at least a night on the town.
But why we need some commitment thing?
Baby, slow it down!

Lazy 'bout books, and seein' movie flicks,
Lazy 'bout the news, so sick 'a politics,
You heard me, baby: let's be lazy in love.

Lazy 'bout my bod, lazy 'bout my brain,
You better not be inhalin',
Cause I'll be sayin:
Lazy 'bout religion,
those people so insane!
Whatever, baby: let's be lazy in love.
Why you gettin' outta bed?
I swear this ain't no fling.
Just need time to think, to sleep,
Can't rush into no such thing.

I'm Lazy 'bout!
I'm Lazy 'bout!
I'm Lazy 'bout!
I'm Lazy 'bout!

I'm lazy 'bout love!
I'm lazy 'bout love!
I'm lazy 'bout love!
I'm lazy 'bout love!
Cause I am L-A-Z-Y,

too lazy to rhyme!!!!

Thursday, 11:52 A.M.

"*'IH 'ej suave*," says Jack Jack.

It's Klingon for *I am handsome and suave*.

"Fuck does that mean?" asks Topper, already knowing.

"*Qo'DaSovchugh, vaj layerteS.*" (Translation: "If you don't know, you're a loser.")

"*Mojpu', vaj vISov, layerteS!*" ("Actually, if I *did* know, I'd be a loser!")

"*qaSlaH jIHbe' virgin!*" ("At least I'm not a virgin.")

"*Hoch nuv 'Iv tlhIngan jatlh virgins, ghobe' ghaHlaw.*" ("I thought all people who spoke Klingon were virgins, no?")

"*Hoch nuv 'Iv tlhIngan jatlh virgins, ghobe' ghaHlaw.*" ("I want to suck your mother's ass.")

"*SoSlI' ass suck vIneH!*" ("At least she has one.")

"Fuck does that means?" asks Jack Jack. (Translation: "*qej Qu'fuck?*")

"Okay, new subject," says Wes, from the pitched roof. He's wearing a T-shirt that reads IT'S NOT GOING TO SUCK ITSELF.

The "NOT" has worn away.

"E.T. has the biggest cock out of all aliens. *Zero* doubt about it. You ever see the size of that fucker's fingers?"

"That's just a rumor," says Spooner, rollerblading past and shooting a puck fashioned from fastfood wrappers into a makeshift net created from white tubing stolen from behind a medical supply store. Hanging from the net is a discarded car deodorizer—a Washington State pine. "Fingers don't equal cock length. If true, George Bush would have a huge one. And he doesn't."

"And how would you know?" asks Cody, seated on top of his garbage can, leisurely smoking a Marlboro. He's wearing a 1920s newsboy cap.

There are at least three more hours until the videostore is open for two.

Rollerblading in a circle and pumping his fist like the rollerblading champion he so desperately wants to be, Spooner says: "I've *seen* it. But I'm going to tell you something, okay? You know which alien has the bigger dick? That mean-ass one from *Alien*, all right?"

Inside Spooner's messenger's bag is an incredibly important document from the mayor to the city's chief of police. Something about an escaped convict. It's been in the bag for three weeks.

"She's a *mother*," says Wes, from above. "Protecting her *baby* alien, you gash-wit."

"She was a *chick*?" asks Jack Jack, barely visible through the misty spritz. "No wonder she was in such a nasty mood all the time."

Willow smiles. She is capturing all of this amazing back-and-forth to present to the world. Really, it would be a crime to keep it only for herself.

"Gorbachev," says Spooner. "*Huge* one. Now that's a fact."

"Had a spot on it," says Jack Jack. "Large birthmark."

"In the shape of what?" asks Wes, laughing.

"An even smaller dick."

Willow turns the camera on herself. Holding it out at arm's length, she begins to spin around and around, all the while narrating: "So this is the latest: Jack Jack likes Becca. You haven't met Becca yet. Becca likes Mac. You haven't met Mac either. Royce likes me but I like Toody. Or I thought I did until yesterday. I also might like Mr. Straight. Mr. Straight likes me. Vicky likes Wes but Wes is gay. No one knows who Wes likes. More than anything, Royce loves being a badass. Skip likes Vicky. Vicky loves *everyone*."

With that obligation out of the way, Willow hits STOP and makes her way into the record store. Behind her, she can hear the boys talking about whether Joanie and Chachi really and truly got it on.

Badum. Badum. Ba. Bum.

The bells over the door ring out the alternative melody.

A fifty-something man is lying on the floor.

Eyes closed, clasping his chest, he gurgles an impossible to decipher utterance.

The man is clutching a CD longbox of the Whitney Houston *Bodyguard* soundtrack.

He appears to be experiencing a heart attack.

Willow strides past the cash register where Skip stands, going over the day's receipts.

"If he were holding a Talking Heads album, would you be ignoring him then?" she asks.

"I'd be calling 9-1-1 as we speak," Skip says,

72

barely looking up. "Hell, I'd be down on the floor *myself*, giving the bastard CPR."

Willow steps over the dying customer and retreats to the back office. She is already fatigued and still has another three hours more of work.

Why does she even have *to work anyway? What is the point of it all? Couldn't MTV just give her the damn money for her amazing, world-changing documentary?*

The office is just as Willow had left it the day before: Covered floor to ceiling with just that *right* amount of music-related chaos. She sits. Time to rest.

Willow hears the front door to the store open and a customer enters.

Heavy stomping.

Closer.

Into the office bursts Vicky. She's wearing a pair of thick club-foot corrective shoes, the latest fashion trend. Her Doc Martens just aren't *chunky* enough.

"C'mon, let's go! You've working too hard!"

Work, work, work. That's all Willow hears!

Granted, it's about *not* working but still …

"Where?" asks Willow. "My recumbent is in the shop. And you don't have a car, either."

"Skip will take us. He *adores* me. He'd do anything to spend time with me."

Toby the Wonder dog barks. He's dressed this morning as the Tony Danza character from *Who's the Boss?* The thick, black sideburns and gold necklace with the Italian horn are a nice touch.

"I suppose," starts Willow. "But I have this gener-

73

ation's greatness to capture on my 10-byte, digital flash-memory card. *Futuristic*."

"Later," says Vicky. "Let's locomote."

Vicky is a smidge overweight, which enables her to say things that the lean and emaciated could never get away with saying—at least on film.

"Let's grab Skip and head out." Vicky grabs a fresh handful of low-fat Snackwells for energy.

They're *healthy* for her.

Toby and Willow follow Vicky back out into the store. The dying man is now in the last clutches of life. Willow wonders if his obituary will mention that "Monkey Gone to Heaven" by the Pixies was playing at the time of his demise.

"Hello, Vicky," says Skip. "You must have walked right past me. Apologies. I was going over today's five receipts. It's been a *good* day."

"You really should move this store to a better developed area," says Vicky. "Away from the Lost Boys. They *cannot* be helping business."

"I want the bare minimum of window shoppers," says Skip, over the muffled cries of the dying man. "I'd rather sell Jesus and Mary Chain to *one* person than sell the *Best of Foreigner* to a *million*."

"Very noble of you," says Vicky.

"I'm a noble man," says Skip. "And I'd love me a noble *woman*."

"Not going to find one here," says Vicky. "We need your car. And for you to drive."

"And where might that be to?" asks Skip loudly. The cries from the customer are only growing brasher and more obnoxious. *Getting out of here for a spell might not be such a bad thing ...*

"Where do you think?" asks Vicky.

If it's anything like last time, Skip already kind of knows where they're headed.

Ten minutes later, Vicky, Willow and Skip sit within their usual booth at the Bean There, their favorite high-end STD clinic and coffee shop.

This remains the only coffee house in town in which everyone born exactly between 1964 and 1983 can relax on cozy, over-stuffed couches and 1950s-style kitchen chairs, while sipping their caffeinated libations in ceramc coffee mugs so large they have their own tidal currents.

Anyone else—older or younger—can only look on with great resentment.

Vicky is in the bathroom taking a pregnancy test.

"When are you going to finally ask Vicky out?" asks Willow.

"She already knows I like her," says Skip.

"She only wants *positive* energy," says Willow. "None of this moping stuff. Be smooth. Talk her up. Say something. *Anything*!"

"I'm not a moper. I'm a *realist*," says Skip. "Top ten songs to prove that I'm a realist, here we go. 'Fade Into You' by Mazzy Star—"

Vicky returns from the bathroom. She throws a hungry glance at the cute guy who is playing the *vielle*, a European bowed stringed instrument popular in the Medieval period.

"*Adorbs*," says Vicky, again joining the table.

"Well?" asks Willow.

"Negativo," replies Vicky. She shrugs.

_N.B.D._

No big deal. grunge slang

"Skip was just about to launch into a fresh list," says Willow.

Vicky looks bored. "Have they called my coffee yet?"

"Not yet," says Willow.

"Irish coffee!" yells the teenage barista. "Negative on the herpes and crabs check! Vicky? _Vicky_?"

"Double plus good news!" says Willow. "You're not pregnant _and_ you're clear of any STDs!"

"Yippy ya yoo," mutters Vicky.

"Shouldn't you be more careful?" says Skip. It's not even a question.

Vicky pretends she's the uptight voice on an answering machine: "At the sound of the beep please leave your name and number, and a brief justification for harping on another person's sex life. _Beeeeep_!" Vicky waits a moment, and then delivers the punchline: "Whoops. _All full_!"

Willow laughs. She can't help it. True, her friend is not skinny and not particularly attractive but she does have a _terrific_ sense of humor.

She has to.

How else would she survive?

Vicky stands and walks over for her Irish coffee. Just another perfectly ordinary day in stagnant, electrifying Seattle.

Two new customers enter the Bean There.

It's Mac and Becca!

This is perfection!

Willow has yet to capture these two amazing characters on camera, even though she's already talked about them in her narration.

She hurriedly waves them over and unloops the Fuji DS-100 digicam with 3-power zoom from her belt. It's just next to her beeper.

"Over *here* guys!" Willow screams. "Time to capture *more* of my generation!"

She turns the camera on Becca and Mac, who stare back blankly.

"C'mon, you two," urges Willow. "*Let's make history!* This will soon be seen by millions! On *MTV*!"

"A musical video?" asks Mac. He's been out of the country far too long. "Is this what you're shooting?"

Mac is wearing logger's clothing, all from Patagonia. *The shirt still pleasantly itches ...*

"No, not a music video," says Willow, spreading her arms wide. "MTV is doing *everything*. *So much more than just music!*"

"Like what?" Becca asks.

"Shows, contests …" says Willow. "Even playing *black* music."

"Public Enemy?" asks Mac. "Wu-Tang?"

"Vanilla Ice," says Willow, a bit defensively. "But at least they're *playing* it, you know?"

"Didn't you date him?" Mac asks Vicky.

"Vanilla Ice?" says Vicky. "No, you're thinking of another white dolt who wore a leather jacket with a stop sign on the back. Sno Topp."

"*Licky licky boom blickety!*" sings Mac. "*White boys got all this here stickity!*"

"Not good," says Vicky sadly. "Regretting that one."

"Thick beats and flash rhymes!" announces Becca.

"More like sad pleats and rash signs," responds Vicky.

"Time for a game!" says Willow. "Let's list every *Gilligan's Island* we know by heart! Vicky, you're *first*!"

"The one where Gilligan acts like an idiot," says Vicky.

"The one where the Mosquitoes play!" says Mac. "I *love* that episode, do you remember it?! They were a band on the island! Song was called 'Don't Bug Me!'"

"Oh! Hey! How about the one where the Professor builds that hanging fuck-chair out of coconuts?" screams Vicky.

"Hanging fuck-chair?" asks Mac.

"Out of coconuts?" asks Becca.

They don't remember this one.

"Okay, now a Sad Off," says Willow. "Saddest stories! *Go!*"

"Um," says Mac. "My dog once died."

"My cat died," offers Becca. "And he wasn't that old either. Just died. That affected me greatly."

"Grandmother died," says Mac.

"Mine, too," says Becca.

"Mine, too," says Vicky.

Now they all truly look sad, not even pretending. But not sad enough for Willow.

"*Sadder*," says Willow. "Like you're *super super super* sad!"

"Hermit crabs died," says Mac. "Names were Donny and Marie."

"Ooofa," says Vicky.

Becca and Mac stare down at their shoes …

"*Sadder*! *Gloomier*!"

"You want us to stare at our shoes in a gloomy way?" asks Mac.

"Yes," says Willow. "Bingo!"

Becca had arrived the previous week from Athens, Georgia, a city moving at too quick a pace. She had heard a rumor that a movie to feature Matt Dillon would soon be shooting in Seattle, and she desperately hoped to earn a walk-on role as a girl dancing inside a club who remarks on the lifelike nature of Matt Dillon's awful wig. movie reference "Singles"

Mac had also arrived the previous week. He has spent the year hiking in the Himalayas in order to shake hands with the Dalai Lama (almost happened, didn't) and a year in Bucharest drinking coffee in outdoor cafes while wearing Oakley glasses (almost didn't happen, did) and a year in India teaching "step aerobics" to the poor (happened, nearly killed).

Time for a fresh change. He now flies the flannel strong.

Next year he intends to head off to grad school to study a dead language. Doesn't matter where, as long as it's been super hyped and the language is nothing but dead.

"Is this better?" asks Mac. He's staring at his shoes,

79

practically weeping.

He's thinking of when he was banned from the library for not returning a few hundred books on time. That affected him terribly.

"I love it!" says Willow.

"I hate myself and want to *die*," says Mac.

"Gorgeous!" says Willow. "And now, if you would, please recite your favorite Ayn Rand quote …"

Skip suddenly lets out a shout.

At first Willow thinks he's come up with a new idea for a list—*top ten songs to think about while others are making lists?*—but, no, his mouth is agape and he's pointing to the store's entrance.

"My god," is all he can say. "It's *him*!"

"*Who?*" asks Vicky, looking over.

"*Him*," says Skip again, still pointing.

Mac grins. "A cager in a noose!"

Translation: *A straight arrow who owns and drives a car and wears a tie.*

Mac's a quick learner when it comes to the grunge speak.

"Not just *any* cager," says Skip, winking. "Willow's very *own* cager."

Walking through the front door is none other than Mr. Straight. And he's headed straight for their table!

A warm and cold front about to collide.

Can Willow and her friends weather this potential storm?

Does this happen in other locations?

Even in cities with better metaphors?

"Mr. Aaron Smith, himself," says Skip. "The one,

80

the *only*!"

"He's cute," whispers Vicky to Willow. "*Not bad at all.* Does he play a medieval instrument?"

"Doubt it," says Mac. "Bet he plays nothing but the stock market."

"Iced coffee!" yells the teenage barista, from behind them. "Negative on the warts! Janey? *Janey*?!"

"May I have a seat?" Mr. Straight asks. Willow notices his tie is different from the tie he was wearing yesterday.

What man her own age actually owns more than one—of anything?

"I've been thinking about our encounter," says Mr. Straight, taking a seat right next to Willow, and staring straight into the camera. His face now fills the entire frame. "How is your ankle?"

"Not bad. Swelling gone way down."

"Good. Again, I apologize. I took it upon myself to have your recumbent bicycle fixed. It's in the shop now."

"What's happening?" asks Mac.

"Seems that Mr. Straight over here hit Willow on his way to work yesterday," says Skip. "Seems that Willow never told anyone but me about it. She told me from a *car* phone. *Secrets*."

"It's no big deal," says Willow, from behind the camera. "I did not even think … it was such a *big deal*."

"Uh huh," says Vicky, sarcastically.

"What are you filming?" asks Mr. Straight. "I noticed the camera when I hit you with my car while

81

looking at my map."

"Capturing my generation," says Willow, with a shrug.

No big deal.

As if.

Mr. Straight looks around the coffee shop. "I've never been here before. But I know that this is the ... *right* place for you types to hang."

"*Types to hang*?" says Becca. "Whoo boy!"

"Well, whatever you guys calls it," says Mr. Straight. "I just know it's popular. And what I'd like to know, Willow, is this … "

Pausing, eyes to the ceiling, he unloosens his tie knot. Eyes back on Willow, he says: "I'd like to know if you'd allow me to take you out for dinner tomorrow night at Lé Chíc."

"*Ooooooh*," says Skip, in a fancy manner. "Only the hippest new restaurant in the city!"

"I heard about that place," says Mac. "It's … *chic*."

"I guess that's why they call it Lé Chíc," says Vicky.

"American food served with a *Continental* twist," says Mac. "Twenty dollars for the extravagant mac and cheese."

"I read about it in *Vanity Fair,* " says Mr. Straight, confidence restored.

The grungers look at each other.

Mainstream.

Optimist.

Dependable.

Lame.

"Was that the issue with Mrs. Doubtfire on the cover?" asks Willow.

"Very exciting," says Mac.

"Indeed," says Mr. Straight, again unaware of the dig.

Who under the age of thirty says "indeed"? thinks Willow.

"Don't know if she can," says Vicky. "We're throwing a Safe Sex party tomorrow night. That's what people our age do these days. It's the Gen X version of an orgy. Join us?"

Willow fires at Vicky a glare. *She is no enemy of drama, this one.*

"Vicky is very much in touch with her sexuality," Willow explains. "And I'm a filmmaker. Hence this camera."

"Safe Sex party?" says Mr. Straight. "I don't know what that is."

Typical. It's only the hottest Gen X style party in Seattle! Or could be. No one's yet been to one.

They've only heard Tori Amos bestow its benefits in Details.

"Partiers come dressed as their favorite prophylactic," explains Vicky. "Or secondary sex characteristics. Or bedroom toys. Or STDs."

"And what's yours?"

"Penis," says Vicky, immediately. No hesitation.

"Sponge," says Willow. "And yours?"

"I ... I suppose the condom?" Mr. Straight is blushing. "But ... I also like the ... vagina?"

Mr. Straight is not used to such straight grunge

talk. Then again, not many are. They will be soon, though. Especially with the help of Willow's upcoming MTV documentary.

"The vagina is not a secondary sex characteristic," said Vicky. "That's a *first* sex characteristic."

"Neither is the *penis*," says Mr. Straight.

Vicky rolls her eyes: "Gas."

"Gas?" asks Mr. Straight. *Some ppl pretend*

"Gives. A. *Shit*?" *not to care but they really do*

"Well ... we can always go to the party and then out to eat?" asks Mr. Straight. "That could be a possibility, right? Um, if that's ... cool?" *Eat Out !?*

Cool? and then maybe ...

"Forgive me," says Willow, "but I didn't formally introduce you to all my friends. Everyone, this is ..." Willow pauses. "Mr. Straight," she finishes, not mentioning his real name. "Mr. Straight, this is *everyone*. And I mean *everyone* in Seattle. Who *matters*."

"Nice to meet you," says Mr. Straight graciously, apparently not taken aback by his new nickname. "Very nice to meet all of you."

"So tell me," says Vicky. "What do you do, Mr. *Straight*?"

"Business," says Mr. Straight. "Finance. Commerce."

All nod.

"And what did you do before Business and Commerce?"

"The Environment."

Willow focuses the camera on her friends' reactions. They've not yet met someone their own age with a work history this incredibly nuanced. It occurs to Willow that she's not yet answered Mr. Straight's question. Then again, there *is* Toody to think about.

But would Toody ever actually *care* if she went out with this yuppie?

Does someone with Toody's great looks ever get jealous?

"What exactly did you do regarding the environment?" asks Mac. "Any special interest?"

"Oh, you know," says Mr. Straight. "*This. That. The other.*"

"What does that mean?" asks Becca.

"One day," he says.

"One day when?" asks Willow.

"Well... one day soon enough, I suppose."

"What else can we talk about?" she asks, flirting. *It feels good.*

"Whatever you want. Do you like golf?"

"Only the Goofy Golf variety," says Willow.

"How about sailing? Drinking expensive wine, watching the sunset?"

"Never been. And I get sea sick."

"I'm sure we can find *something*," he says, smiling broadly. "That we *both* can enjoy. *Mutually.*"

His teeth. *So white.*

Willow is more used to the grunge mouth. Gums aflame, teeth gone a'lame.

"Meet me 7:00 tomorrow night," says Willow. "Probably no dinner after but we can party."

"Great!" answers Mr. Straight, standing. "I assume I'll pick you up at that building where everyone cool in Seattle lives? The building where I dropped you off? With the water fountain? And the freight elevator? People smoke and gossip in front? They wear black? A sign outside reads *SINGLES AVAILABLE*? It could very well have a double meaning? That place?"

"Correct," says Willow, impressed. "But the party is at the record store."

A look of fear crosses Mr. Straight's eyes.

Danger! Painful! Avoid!

Mr. Straight shoots Skip a look. Skip ignores it.

"Okay then," says Mr. Straight, trying to act nonplussed.

But fake enthusiasm is not his best fit. "Well, it was nice to meet all of you. Nice place here. Do they have decaf? I prefer decaf. Or a nice tea."

He waits for an answer that does not arrive. And continues:

"Okay, cool as school! Willow, I shall see *you* tomorrow."

Cool as school?!

He retreats.

"Why don't you just sleep together, get married, break up, get engaged again, obtain a marriage license, break up, get back together, and then divorce already?" asks Vicky, watching Mr. Straight stiffly walk out.

"I didn't know you were dating Ross Perot," says Mac.

"More boring than that Ken Burns documentary on ... " What was that documentary again? Becca tries to think. "The late-night talk-show wars?"

Mac laughs.

- shampoo
- razors
- eggs

In a deep, professional narrator's voice, he breaks into the following: "*Dearest darling. Indications are very strong that we shall engage tomorrow night with Mister Jay Leno. And lest I shall not be able to write you again, I write so today. I have no misgivings about the task of which I am stoutly gauged. O, yet I forge on. Yours. Mister David Letterman.*"

"Cappuccino!" yells the teenage barista, from behind them. "Positive on the HPV! Mac? *Mac*?!"

"Shit," says Mac. He stands to retrieve his drink. "Knew I shouldn't have slept with that Russian."

Skip shakes his head. "That's what I've been trying to say all along about this guy. Why haven't you listened to me? Mr. Straight is a dullard."

"Then why don't you say it?" asks Vicky.

Skip shrugs. Maybe one day he will. For now, there's a fresh list to create. Specifically: the order of the sub-genres of music he enjoys the most, starting from those he likes the least:

Classic rock. Cock rock. Grunge. Fratboy funk. Trashcore ....

"There's just *something* about him," says Willow.

"Isn't Toody coming to the party tomorrow night?" asks Vicky.

"Yes," says Willow.

"And? How will you handle *this* one?" asks Vicky.

Willow reaches to the heavens in a "giving up" gesture, like something you'd see in a movie about twenty-somethings written by fifty-somethings.

"He probably won't! And if he does, I'll figure it out then! Besides, *you* mentioned the party! I didn't!

Thanks for that one."

Willow hates when things *happen*. It's so much more exciting and intriguing when things *don't* happen. But when events *have* to happen, she supposes, you just have to *deal* with them. *You're an adult now.* But, by god, how she wishes she were back in college, doing nothing all day and so very little in the evenings and not wanting anything else out of life!

Not this... *madness.*

Snide rock. Redneck thrash. Ambient synth. Ska revival. Jazz rock. Jizz rock. Jock rock...

"Aren't you already dating someone who pays zero attention to you?" asks Vicky.

No-wave. No-core. Acid pop. Math rock. Art punk. Britpunk ....   *knows more about rock than relationships*

"I love Toody, I really do. But ..."

Post rock. Pre-rock. DC Punk. LA Punk. Minnesota punk. New progressive. Classic progressive.

Skip finishes his list, at long last, and promptly falls asleep. He's exhausted. He dreams of hugging Lee Mavers of The La's and pleading for a second album.

" ... but," finishes Willow, "well, Toody has been a bit aloof these past few days."

Willow flashes back to how she and Toody first met, the previous week, between sets at the Re-Bar, Toody casually doodling his band's mascot on a bar napkin. It was the word *Anarchy*, with the A in the shape of the Seattle Space Needle. Willow was shy but pushed through, regardless. College was behind her and adulthood was before her now and anything could happen and anything *would* happen—*she'd*

88

make sure of that.

"I liked your show," Willow had said to Toody.

"Thank you."

"Does your band play any instruments?"

"Not yet."

"You're cute."

"I know."

"Wanna make out?"

"Yes."

The next day, Toody took Willow out on their first official date, to the gravesite of Jimi Hendrix and they made love as fans dropped flowers and cigarette butts on Toody's bare ass. It was the perfect manner in which to lose one's virginity (Willow's). Toody had lost his years ago, behind a ROCK THE VOTE booth at a Cinderella concert at the Capitol Centre, in Largo, Maryland, long before ever going grunge.

Even his pubic hair had been sprayed and teased.

Willow desperately wants to remain loyal to someone as special as Toody but there's just *something* about this new one, Mr. Straight, that she can't stop thinking about.

Maybe it's all his adult neckties? Or his office cubicle with a stuffed Jimmy Buffett parrothead doll to signify that fun actually exists somewhere out in the real world amongst middle-aged alcoholics who like to party at Margaritavilles in suburban office parks by getting smashed and eating microwaved frozen shrimp for $18?

Mr. Straight had told Willow that he absolutely adores Jimmy Buffett. Not only because he's a great artist.

But also because he's a great *businessman*.

Willow is at a loss to explain her attraction to the dark side. "I don't know. It might just be that he apologizes after he farts," says Willow to Vicky now. "Toody doesn't. Mr. Straight doesn't have to speak through a distortion box to sound interesting. Besides, whatever Toody doesn't know, won't hurt Toody. So we'll see."

Here, at the table inside the Bean There, this gang of twenty-somethings' favorite high-end STD clinic and coffee shop, things quickly get back to normal.

Skip snoozes away.

Willow shoots on.

Becca fills out a crossword in the favorite free alt weekly *The Rocket*:

What's a six-letter word for "anguish"?

No problem!

How about a seven-letter word for "discontent"?

Yup, ya got it!   petulant!

How about an eight-letter word for "petulant"?

Ain't no thang!

This week's puzzle is particularly fun and easy!

Mac is still up at the front counter arguing over his poor test results with Jenesis, the barista. But Jenesis is not budging. She's wearing a *Huipil*, the most common "traditional" garment worn by indigenous women from central Mexico to Central America. She bought it at the Salvation Army.

Meanwhile, and for no apparent reason—or perhaps for a very good reason, known only to her—

Vicky breaks into a spirited rendition of "Conjunction Junction":

Conjunction Junction, what's your function?
Hooking up words and phrases and clauses! ...

Vicky finishes one of her favorite childhood songs but then launches into a set of improvised lyrics. The song turns into the tale of how she had once applied to work right here in the Bean There but was unfairly and dishonorably not hired because of a resume written in crayon on the back of a stained placemat from Burger King.

Fucking draconian Boomer mentality bullshit assholery!

Skip suddenly awakes from his afternoon snooze with a high-pitched scream.

"Dream pop!" he yells. "*Dream! POP!*"

Everyone at the table laugh very hard, especially Vicky.

As they'll later find out, Skip had been dreaming of making love to Hope Sandoval of Mazzy Star on a public beach. The town council had shut down the beach for the entire day to give these two special lovers the privacy they so desperately craved.

It was a nice dream and a wonderful nap, and Skip heads on back to it. Maybe this go-round he can dream about fucking Kim Deal from the Breeders?

Will the authorities be willing to close the public beach for this one?

Willow zooms in closer on her table of friends. She does not want to miss a single solitary incident. It is all just too valuable—in an *historical* sense.

she wants to capture posterity like any other **91** but she just happens to her own time for early 20-something live in the 1990s

Friday, 9:47 P.M.

Inside the record store, the "Safe Sex" party is going quasi-hard.

Meanwhile, outside in the misty rain, the Lost Boys are where they always are, in the parking lot, where they "hang."

Spooner, the potential rollerblading champion of Seattle, is wearing a dental dam costume—a large piece of rubber stretched over his face, making it all that much more difficult to successfully navigate on his blades.

Jack Jack is dressed as one tremendously large condom. He's holding a bag of take-out Chinese. "Ribs, y'all," he announces. "For *my* pleasure."

Cody is truly feeling the grunge spirit. Too lazy to breathe through the aid of a sleep apnea mask, Cody now lies within a rented iron lung, and allows the contraption to do the breathing *for* him.

He's smoking a Marlboro, shoulder-length green hair now pink. The iron lung is bedecked as a gigantic dildo.

Wes—gay and recently "out"—is still on the gabled roof. In honor of his significant protest against homophobia, he is *not* costumed as a form of birth control or a first- or secondary-sex characteristic. He's still in his graduation gown.

Wes is talking with Bake about a very important subject: *Who gets laid the most? Superheroes who* fly *or superheroes who* swim?

They all wait anxiously for the inventor of the hacky sack with the new South African colors to arrive.

They don't want to miss such an iconic event!

He will show! How could he not? What else could he possibly do but visit old pals in the parking lot where he used to "chill" before he just up and left to become a super success?

"Say that again," Royce says, chewing languidly on a plastic straw.

Royce, the badass of the bunch, is just back from a place called "Iraq."

He has the color and complexion of a red-pebbled-drinking-glass at a Pizza Hut.

Willow, from behind the camera: "And if you could say it even just a *little* louder and towards the camera, that'd be *super*!"

"Superheroes who fly get laid the *most*," Royce barks. "Those who swim? The *least*."

"You don't think Aquaman gets laid?" asks Topper, speeding past on his black board, jumping off the curb and performing a 360, landing at the very spot from which he launched, as if nothing was ever attempted and nothing was ever gained.

Perfection.

The ideal trick.

"Why would you *not* want to sleep with someone who flies?" asks Wes. "You'd rather fuck someone who smells of brackish water and gulf shrimp?"

"The first gay superhero was Batman," says Mac,

93

his fisherman's cap moist with dew. At least everyone *hopes* it's dew. "No one—and I mean, *no one*—wore leather like Batman."

"Disagree," says Wes. "*Superman* was the first homosexual superhero. *Think about it!* He came from a different planet with gorgeous ice sculptures and beautiful designs and he leaves and travels to a land in the middle of a drab field, totally alone. Why? *To add some color to earthlings' lives!"*

"*New* topic. Gay robots!" says Mac. "Kicking it off: R2D2 was definitely gay!"

He slaps a shot into a makeshift net. The puck is a melted-down hard VHS case from the video store.

"So was C3PO," says Wes. "Any robot who talks with an English accent is gay."

"Not Rutger Hauer in *Blade Runner*." It's Spooner.

"Wasn't a robot. Was a *replicant*. And it wasn't a British accent." It's Bake. Or Wake? Christ. *Which one was which again? Does it even matter?*

"One thing for sure," says Royce. "Han Solo was definitely never gay. Dude killed Greedo because of a woman. That crazy space pussy just *that* hot to handle!"

"Han killed Greedo because Greedo shot first," said Mac.

"Other way around," says Wes, from the roof. "It was Han who shot Greedo *before* Greedo was intending to *shoot* Han."

"I just want to know who had to clean up the mess," says Spooner, rollerblading backwards and performing a lazy figure 2. He shoots a plastic cup into a trash can and roars as if a very large crowd is nearby. "All that *blood* and *gore* inside that cantina."

"Cantina bus boy," says Wes. "I'd love to know how much that idiot earned per hour."

"Wonder if recessions exist in space?" It's Spooner. "If the economy sucks up there too."

"In space, no one can hear you declare bankruptcy," says Royce, lighting up a Marlboro.

"Wonder if there are temp agencies in space?" It's Mac.

In an hilarious, officious voice, Spooner booms: "Hi. This is the Intergalactic Temp Agency! We are calling to inquire as to whether you might be open to working as a cantina bus boy. You will need your own X-wing to commute *to* and *from* the job. Lunch is 30 minutes, unpaid. If interested, please communicate with our home office on Cloud City!"

Now they all join in:

"Hey, space temp! Sweep up this Wookie shit!"

"Hey, space temp! Got a message I want deliered to Darth! Just barge right into his office! Darth adores surprises!"

"Hey, space temp! Ewok just got run over! Go buy a fresh one at the pet store!"

The pay phone rings. Wake picks the phone off the receiver. He taps the phone once for "yes" just like Wake would do.

95

"Hello?" says a voice on the other end.

Wake again taps the phone for yes.

"Hello? Anyone *there*?" asks the voice. "Hello?!"

Wake drops the phone. Royce picks up the receiver and asks: "Define irony or I'll *kill* you."

"Hello?" says the voice on the other end. "*Who is this?*" BIG question in early 90s

Royce makes the game-show buzzer sound for "wrong answer."

"Please!" the voice says.

Royce whistles the tune for Final Jeopardy.

"You must define irony or I'm hanging up," Royce says eventually.

"Is Willow there, please?" asks the voice.

Male. Mainstream. No time for fun. Smells like Boomer ...

"Willow!" yells Royce. "It's your dad! *Hooya!*"

"I'm more interested in what the urinals in that cantina bathroom smelled like," announces Cody, leaning against the record store brick wall. "Can you imagine?"

"I can try," Wes says.

"Willow!" yells Royce again from the pay phone. "It's your dad!"

Willow shakes her head no.

She's too busy capturing the genius of her generation. Maybe later.

"Just send another rent check," says Royce into the phone, and hangs up.

"I'd love another *Star Wars*!" says Cody. "How *amazing* would that fucking be?!"

96

"God, I hope there'll be at least one more *Star Wars*!" says Royce. "It would be the best fucking movie in the entire universe! It would just be so so so *so amazing*! Imagine what Lucas could *do* with *today's* technology!"

"*Computer* technology!" adds Wes, not knowing what this means but knowing it sounds mighty impressive.

Becca is on the ground, playing Dejarik, the board game seen aboard the Millennium Falcon in *Star Wars: A New Hope*. Her opponent is Mac.

Instead of tiny, moving holographic creatures, they're using scraps of trash found in the parking lot.

"Without a doubt," says Mac, moving one of his plastic sporks and attacking one of Royce's plastic straws. "*Computer! Technology!*"

Royce, back from the pay phone, nods. "Yeah, that'd be cool. But why stop there? How about a new *Indiana Jones*? How great would *that* fucking be?!"

"That's it for now!" yells Willow, to her friends, pressing the STOP button on her Fuji DS-100 digi-cam. "See y'all soon!"

Time for *work*.

Her much-needed break is over. Now it's back to partying.

The Safe Sex party is in deep, dank Seattle swing. The record store is filled with hundreds of men and women dressed as various forms of birth control, not to mention first- and secondary-sex characteristics.

And lively and vibrant STDs.

It seems that *everyone* in Seattle of a certain age

is here tonight!

Skip is dressed as one very large pubic crab. Felt pincers. Plastic antennae. Ping Pong balls for eyes.

"Top five songs about sex," says Skip to a very attractive woman dressed as a suppurating herpes sore. She's standing next to her friend, dressed as a bottle of Kwell. "Let's start it off with 'Laid' by James. Okay. So then it's off to the races with 'Lips like Sugar' by Echo and the Bunnymen. 'Kiss Off' by the Violent Femmes would come just behind. What else? *What else, damnit?!* ..."

"Hey," says Willow to Vicky, strolling up and hugging her. Vicky is decked out as an IUD, but with factory pre-ripped jeans. "So glad you're here. And guess what? Your hair smells *terrific*."

Vicky smiles. She gets the reference. She *always* gets the reference. *commercial at the time*

"And I'm glad *you* are here," says Vicky. "Wonder if I'll get pushy-pumped tonight? I have a Swedish headache that needs some curing!" *she wants*

"I think there's a very good chance." *to have sex*

"And yet I have that 'not so fresh feeling,'" says Vicky.

Willow laughs extremely hard. Another amazing reference! *This time to a 1970s douche commercial!*

Vicky doesn't return the laugh.

Maybe it is not a reference.

Maybe it's just a fact.

"I really love your outfit," says Vicky. "See! I *told* you it would work!"

It was Vicky's idea to dress Willow as descended

testicles.

Actually, Willow is dressed as just *one* descended testicle.

The other testicle remains *ascended* because it's too difficult for Willow to walk with both scraping the floor.

"Have you been watching the door?" asks Willow.

"I have, yes … when not observing all the genitals and sores. Whoo boy. I think this Safe Sex party might just fall into the category of 'better in theory.'"

Willow laughs. They have an entire list. "Like picnics."

"Or piano bar dates."

"Like playing Cheap Trick on your crush's answering machine."

"Onion loafs."

"Air mattresses."

"Complimentary continental breakfasts."

"Dry humpin'."

"Destination weddings."

"Fake snow."

"Giving a shit."

"Yeah," says Willow. "Giving a shit."

"Yeah," agrees Vicky. "Amen, sister. Giving a shit."

"Have either showed yet?" Willow asks. "Toody or Mr. Straight?"

"Not yet," says Vicky. "Unless they were the suppurating skin blisters who entered earlier. Or the guys with the jesters' hats dressed as gonorrhea discharge."

"Not likely," says Willow, placing her Fuji digicam back on her stone-washed belt-loop on her distressed jeans. "I *love* this film that's showing!"

She points to the movie screens placed all around the store. On them, a locally-shot and -produced porn film called *Busy Doin' Nothin'* can be seen: a young man in untucked flannel goes door-to-door to collect money for environmental causes. After he collects, he lazily avoids fucking and goes back to collecting.

The *quintessential* Gen X pornography.

Vicky has slept with five of the actors. And three of the actresses. And the director. And the producer, a sixty-three-year-old logger from Takoma named Burt.

Vicky watches the herpes sore walk away from Skip, the pubic lice. "Poor Skip! Guy has *zero* game."

"Buried under a layer of insecurity and shyness masked with pathetic lists, he's not such a bad guy," says Willow about her boss of five days.

"You really think so?" asks Vicky.

After a long pause, "No."

Both laugh.

At the entrance to the store, Toby the Wonder Pooch is resting. He barely looks up when Toody enters. Not that he can. The poor thing is made to look exactly like a cock ring.

"Here we go," Willow says.

Behind Toody comes Mr. Straight. He also steps over Toby.

"Here we *double* go," says Vicky.

Toody arrives first.

"Pubic thatch?" asks Vicky.

"Huh?" Toody asks through the super-fuzz distortion box that he carries around via a shoulder strap.

"On your face."

"Very funny," Toody says.

He gently strokes his soul patch. Granted, it *does* look like a vagina. He has one yellow ear plug inserted into his right nostril. As hard as he's working it, this trend has yet to catch on.

"I forgot I had to dress up. Would rather be practicing."

"Practicing what?" asks Vicky. "You guys do nothing!"

"Nothing?! We *grunge prance*! Not as easy as it looks. Hey, Willow! What are you dressed as? Two sweet yams with the sprouts still attached?"

"Um, no actually—" starts Willow before being interrupted by the arrival of Mr. Straight.

His cologne arrives before his actual presence.

"'Sup, cups?" he states.

Sup, cups?!

He's wearing his typical business-appropriate outfit, save for a funny looking tie.

"I love your tie," says Vicky. She shoots a look over to Willow as if to say: *See? I told you they would both show. Now what are you going to do?*

"Thanks!" says Mr. Straight. "It's made out of condoms. They're just taped on. Didn't know what else to do." He reaches out to Toody. "Hi. My name is Kevin. It's nice to meet you. I didn't see you yesterday at the Bean There." out of his element

Vicky sings the theme song to *The Twilight Zone*.

101

She does this whenever a situation becomes unbear-ably awkward.

It's very funny and extremely effective.

"Likewise," says Toody, barely taking Mr. Straight's hand. The last thing he needs is a bruised mic hand.

Especially with the great Grunge Off coming up …

"Are you a music exec?" Toody asks. "Cause you look like one."

"Ha, no! I'm just working on finance matters! In a regular old office downtown. Nothing too rock and roll, I'm afraid!"

"So what do you stand for?"

"What do you mean?"

"What's your purpose? What's your *reason* for being?"

"I … I don't understand the question."

"What I'm *asking*," says Toody, adjusting his ear plug in his right nostril, "what I'm asking is this: *greed*. Is it good?"

"I believe that an open market creates the most fertile soil for a nation to grow and prosper," says Mr. Straight.

Toody looks confused. "I'm just asking if greed is good. Yes or no."

Mr. Straight smiles. "And what might your opin-ion of the Keynesian economy philosophy be? An *increase* or *decrease* in government expenditure?"

"Asshole," Toody seethes through a tight smile.

"Nice to meet you, too," says Mr. Straight. And then, turning to Willow: "Dinner after this?"

She smiles at Mr. Straight. Toody catches it.

"I see," Toody says. "Gone over to the dark side. Where you two headed?"

"Not sure yet," says Mr. Straight.

"I was just about to ask you, Willow," says Toody, "if you'd like to come out with *me* for some grub." He bats his eyelashes.

"Not sure about tonight, Toods. Why all of a sudden available? I thought you had practice later?"

"Was thinking *before* practice," says Toody. "But you know what? Go fuck your new friend. What do I care?"

"I think you *do* care," says Mr. Straight. "Oh, I really think you *do*."

"Really?" asks Toody. "You *do*?"

"Yes," says Mr. Straight. "In fact, I *know* it. I can read people. It's my *business*."

"Let's see about that," says Toody. "Let's just *see* about that."

Willow, Vicky and Mr. Straight watch Toody strut away. *Where is he headed? What does he have planned?*

He really is a good strutter, admits Vicky to herself. *Maybe he does have that special X Grunge Factor.*

"His name is *Toods*?" asks Mr. Straight. He seems more bemused than annoyed.

"*Toody*. But I call him Toods."

"Is he homeless?"

"Underemployed."

"Are you an item?"

An item?

103

"I don't know," says Willow. "We've been going out for over a week … but these past few days have been a little … *rough*."

"Why didn't you tell me about him earlier?"

"Earlier when? We just met."

"Things move fast in Seattle when they have to," mumbles Vicky.

Willow performs an exaggerated shrug. She's been practicing. She hopes she nails the insouciance she wishes to achieve. It's not as easy as Toody makes it out to be.

Mr. Straight says: "Willow, I think I mentioned Lè Chic last night. I hope this isn't too forward but—"

He pauses. He wants to get this right.

I masturbated to an image of you while on the way over here.

No. That won't do.

Even someone as artsy as Willow wouldn't fully appreciate that.

Start over …

"Willow," Mr. Straight says. "I hope this isn't too forward but I did take the liberty and initiative to make a reservation at Lè Chic. In fact," he looks at his Rolex watch, "in twenty minutes. Would you join me? I'd absolutely *love it* if you did."

"I … I don't know if I can," Willow says, searching the party for where Toody strutted off to.

"Think about it," says Mr. Straight.

"Oh no," says Willow, pointing.

"What?" asks Mr. Straight.

Feedback can be heard over the store's speakers.

All turn to the front, by the door, where Toody stands before a microphone stand.

"*Poetry slam!*" Toody says into the mic, taking it out of the stand. "*Me* versus *that* guy!"

He points to Mr. Straight.

"What's happening?" asks Mr. Straight.

"He's challenging you to a poetry slam."

"Meaning what?"

The STDs and secondary sex characteristics gather before Toody. A nipple hair cheers wildly. A syphilitic penis pumps her tight fist.

Toody launches right into it.

"Business*man*," raps Toody. "Business*man* with *zero* plan. Too *straight* to *create*. Uppity! Yippity! *Yop*! Diggity diggity *hop*!"

"Speaking the truth," someone mutters.

"Outrageous," agrees another. "*Killer*."

"You feel what I'm sayin'? I'm not *playin'*! I stand like a boxer at *weigh*-in! Come on and take a *punch*! But, I tell ya, I got a *hunch*! You running away like a *chooch*, 'fraid of this *crunch*!"

Toody drops his mic. He seems very pleased with himself.

The crowd breaks into a chant: "Too-*dy!* Too-*dy!* Too-*dy!* Too-*dy!* Too-*dy!*"

Toody takes a bow.

"Now what?" asks Mr. Straight.

"Well, if you wanted, you could respond," says Willow.

"Up there?"

"Yes."

"In rhyme?"

"Would probably help."

Mr. Straight shrugs. He walks over to the mic stand and picks out the microphone.

He clears his throat. And takes a long, deep breath.

Willow looks over to Vicky. Both can't believe this is happening. They had never heard of such a thing in college.

Mr. Straight clears his throat. And launches into it: "It's quite simple, really. What we have here is a very desirable, very beautiful, very intelligent woman—"

He points to Willow.

"And two men who are competing for her hand. One appears to have *slithered* forth from a swamp. The other is new to this … *world*, but is more than willing to learn. And willing to put in the time. That's all I have to say. Have fun."

Mr. Straight carefully places the mic back into the stand.

There's no applause but Vicky and Willow exchange a look: It's official. The first poetry-slam performance to ever feature the word "slithered." And to *not* feature a mic drop.

Not bad, Vicky shrugs. *Not bad at all. Maybe this guy's straightness isn't such a liability … maybe it could inadvertently work …*

Willow looks around for Toody's reaction. Where is he? He couldn't have left so quickly, could he?— *no, there he is.* In the corner, flirting with an adorable syphilitic foreskin.

To be a fly on the wall for that non-conversation …

Kevin approaches. "Well, how'd I do?"

"Not bad," says Willow. "Next time, maybe more hand flourishes? And actually rap instead of lecture?"

"Consider it done. Have you thought about dinner?"

"Actually, you know what, Kevin? Screw it … I'm *in*!" says Willow.

"Very nice," says Mr. Straight.

*"How did you know I would say *yes*?"* asks Willow.

"I didn't," answers Mr. Straight, smiling. "See, if you had said *no*, I just would have cancelled from the cellular car phone inside my car. Easy peasy."

Easy peasy?!

Mr. Straight straightens his condom tie and flashes a wide smile. "Anyway, I'm *so* glad."

"I am, too. But I have to tell Toody goodbye."

"You mean, *Toods*," he says. "Okay. I'll wait right here …"

Willow makes her way through the crowd, passing a woman dressed as a mature female peacock's flashy plumage.

Willow should have thought of that one. It'd be a lot easier to drag around.

"Toody," she says. "Toody? I—"

The syphilitic foreskin interrupts: "Um, *excuse* me? Like *who* are you? And why are you *here*? You look like a malignant tumor!"

"Descended testicles," replies Willow, a bit curt. "Or maybe you've never actually seen a pair, *live* and up *close*."

"I've seen *many* malignant tumors up close—" she begins. "And even some on testicles—"

Toody comes between them.

"Just calm down! All three of you!" he screams through the distortion box. "This is Willow. She's my … she's my … um, she's my …"

"I'm your *what*?" asks Willow. "What *exactly* am I to you, Toody?"

"You're my Willow," Toody replies, proudly. "Right? I mean … just … good ol' Willow! How'd I do before? Did I *slam* him?"

"Did you 'slam' him?!" Willow asks. "Did you even hear a word of what Kevin said up there?"

"Not worth my time." He points to his right ear, the plug now within it. "Didn't *wanna* hear it."

"Just good ol' Willow," Willow says, letting her second testicle descend to the ground. *Let it scrape! She no longer cares.* "Well, good ol' Willow is headed out to a dinner date with a man who isn't good ol' Toody!"

Toody attempts to digest this. He strokes his facial pubic thatch. He's still mentally digesting. Conceivably, it could take as long the thousand-year-digestive cycle of Jabba the Hut.

"Why?" he finally. "Why you leaving?"

"Why I leaving? Because he likes me. And he pays *attention* to me."

"He's a lamestain," he says. "A *twinkle-dink*."

That's a new one. *There must be a fresh New York Times article about grunge slang that was just published …*

108

"He very well might be a *twinkle-dink*," says Willow, looking over to Mr. Straight, who's appears to be making small talk with a woman dressed as sexual abstinence. Willow recognizes her as Vyvyan, two 'v's, two 'y's. She looks miserable. To be fair, it's a difficult costume to pull off. "But Kevin is *nice* to me. And he *does* pay attention to me. Unlike *you*."

"Rock and roll," says Toody. "*Waaaaaaaaaaaaaaant to appear tormented!!*"

"Rock and roll," says Willow. "Good luck with your *tormentttttttttttt*."

She marches back towards Mr. Straight, still conversing with the miserable woman holding the ABSTINENCE sign.

"Business," he's saying to her. "And before that *Finance* and *Commerce*. So, Vyvyan, yeah. What I do is *kinda* important."

Abstinence gives a half-hearted, limp thumb's up. She shrugs and leaves to talk with her friend, the vibrating egg.

"Dinner," says Willow. "*Now*."

Willow takes Mr. Straight by his elbow and leads him through the crowd and outside into the parking lot.

The Lost Boys, all in their usual positions in the parking lot, immediately make a "wha-*whoooooooooo*!" noise.

In the mist, like a troop of gorillas, the Lost Boys signify sexual excitement by hooting and hollering just like the sitcom audiences from their favorite Fox TV shows.

Willow leaving with a new man! Now they're getting into his BMW! Has Toody gotten too grunge for her? Is this new guy taking his lumber jack to her wood town? What is happening here?

This is new and exciting!

They see Mr. Straight's BMW reverse and then quickly pull out of the lot.

From the roof, Wes says, "*Quick!* What *Breakfast Club* character does this guy remind you of?"

"The nerd," says Spooner.

Jack Jack, still dressed as a pre-used condom, announces through the reservoir tip, "The janitor."

It all comes out very fast.

"The guy who drops his kid off in the Chevy LeBaron," says Cody, from his iron dildo.

"I *loved* that character!" says Jack Jack. "Always felt so bad for him!"

"The guy alone in his bedroom, listening to Kate Bush all night," says Wes from the roof.

"That was *you*," says Cody.

"No shit," says Wes. "Letting my gay flag *fly*!"

"Only at *half* mast," retorts Cody.

"Well then … if we're going to play that game … the guy who once jerked off to the SunMaid raisin mascot," says Jack Jack. "That was *me*!"

"Worst people you ever jerked off to!" screams Wes, from the roof. "*Go!*"

"Mary Chestnut!" says Mac. "From the Civil War doc."

"Three men," says Wes. "But not the baby!"

"Mary Lou Retton!" screams Jack Jack. "Would

love to stick a 10.0 landing on those mounds!"

"Joe Camel!" says Wes. "Loved that *hump*!"

"Tattoo from *Fantasy Island*!" says Cody. "*De pussy! De pussy!*"

"*New* subject!" Wes screams from the roof. "Worst places you've ever j'ed off! Go!"

"The back of Mr. Willington's history class!" says Cody.

"The *front* of Mr. Willington's history class!" yells Spooner, sipping on a Fruit Gusher from the Convenience Mart.

The boys settle in for the night.

It looks to be a *fantastic* one.

joe camel's nose looks a dick

111

Willow's Fuji DS-100 digicam with 3-power zoom!

Is there anything cooler than *Star Wars*? The Lost Boys don't think so!

"Hello and welcome to the Inconvenience Mart! My name is Topper. Looking for rolling papers?"

Seattle's hottest new dessert: the chocolate lava cake!

The public pay phone

"Fine. I'll wait."

I'd wait for you?!!

"I don't know. Just life and shit, y'know?"

Grunge ain't nothin' but LOVE misspelled!

Word!

Po-Jo to Go Jams It Out to the Go-Go to the Get-Now of
the Future Urban Dance Squad!

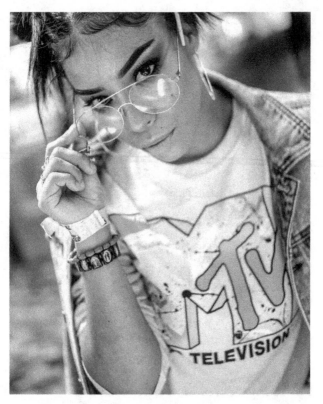

EVERYONE loves their MTV!

The Vickster is a sucker for the swing dance craze!

Ain't no tear like a pre-fabricated tear!

Willow getting ready for her big date at the power lines!

I heard *dat*!

Betz dreams of becoming a seamstress for the grunge band!

"Here I am, Toody! *Ravish* me!"

Who needs an official license to fly?!

[Note for production: DO NOT RUN PHOTO!
She will sue!]

Uh oh! I got me a really bad case of Who Gives a Shit!

See ya, old Seattle! It's time for a fresh sound in town …
grunge!

Seattle's iconic "Space Needle"!

Come watch fish be thrown and laugh yourself silly!

I've been there!!

"I ain't leaving this roof till homosexuality is acceptable to everyone!"

"My major? Apathy? What do you got?!"

Skip's fancy downtown office!

The fountain outside the building where the young, single
people live

THE place to be! Seattle in '93!

"Iraq, man. It was crazy."

A Seattle brewsky with some fresh suds!

Any hot movie you need can be found at Video Plus!

I miss video stores!

Twenty-nine and feelin' fine!

Ain't no ones or zeros in this type of music!

The Doritos skateboarding ad as seen on MTV!

looks like the back room of the pizza place I work at

↓

"It's no stronger than a coffee buzz."

Rain. Seattle's "sunshine."

Insouciance in the key of D

Toody

"Me? Just thinking how lucky I am to be in Seattle in the early 1990s."

The classic rock party that quickly grows out of control!

Even kids are getting into the "Grunge Scene"!

"Sit and spin" ↑

Prof. Doherty's Uncle

The tattoo on Vicky's inner thigh

"What you lookin' at, Grunger?!"

Saturday, 12:01 A.M.

"Oh, my! Was *that* delicious," proclaims Mr. Straight, leaning back in his upholstered restaurant chair.

Lé Chic has lived up to its colossal, modernist name.

"I didn't read about this restaurant in *Vanity Fair*. I *just* remembered! It was rated very highly in *Zagat's*. Have you heard about *Zagat's*? I *adore* it! This place is all fives. Except no fireplace, which kind of sucks. Or a heated backyard patio where one can smoke cigars. But to have both of those amenities, well … that's *rare*! I've only seen it *once*!"

"Ah," says Willow.

Mr. Straight reaches into his dinner jacket's pocket. He pulls out a wrapped gift. "I have a gift for you. It's nothing, really."

Please don't be a ring, Willow thinks. She hates gold and despises the subjugation of the hundreds, or however many they are, forced to work more than a few hours a week, or however many hours, in the African mines, or wherever the hell country they're located. There was once a *Quincy* episode about this.

Silver on the other hand …

"I made you a mix. From songs I really enjoy listening to …"

Willow smiles. *Ah, a cassette mix!* Toody's never done this for her. True, he did once hobble together a

156

mix but it was just ninety minutes of himself scream-ing: "*Are* you ready to rock?! Are *you* ready to rock?! Are you *ready* to rock?! *Are* you ready *to* rock?!"

"This is ... so *nice*," says Willow, glancing at the song titles. In the past, whenever Willow received a mixed tape from a potential suitor, the insert has always been marked from top to bottom in pen with cute drawings, funny sayings, cool quotes from sitcoms.

Not this time.

Willow sees there are just song titles. She can see in neat handwriting: "Don't Worry Be Happy." She sees "Fast Car" by Tracy Chapman. She sees "Never Tear Us Apart" by INXS. She sees "A Groovy Kind of Love" by Phil Collins. She sees "Crazy Love Vol. II" from *Graceland*.

At this point, and feeling a little woozy, she places the tape in her purse.

"Gosh," she says. "*Wow*."

How to exude appreciativeness? Okay, she thinks. *Just improvise! Feign glee! It's totally against every-thing that you currently stand for but sometimes you just have to ... fudge the truth, right?*

"This is so … wow! Stupendous! I cannot wait to listen to these songs! Incredibly *awesome*! *Thank* you, Kev!"

"Aw, it's nothing," he responds. "I just wanted you to know what I liked. Was listening to, I guess. I know it's not as ... expert as what you listen to in a *record* store and all—"

Willow must keep this tape away from Skip and

Vicky and the Lost Boys! She'll never hear the end of it ...

" ... Maybe we can play it together in the car on the ride home," he happily suggests. "And play it a little *loud*?"

"That would be *great*, Kevin. Again, thank you." She places the tape in her purse, hoping to never see it again, at least in the light of day, what little transpires in Seattle, at least according to Hollywood standards.

"What were you saying before? About wanting a house?"

"Ah, yes. I want to buy a house. My own. That's my life goal. I live in an duplex now, alone. I want something in the suburbs. With a fence. And a lawn."

Willow tries to imagine herself standing on a lawn, next to a fence, waving at neighbors. She can't. She tries again. *Why can't she do this?* Okay, one more time ...

No.

Kevin fiddles with his puce-colored cloth napkin. "I'd like to continue working in the business field, you know. And ... I'd like to, I don't know, let my hair down a little. Have some fun. Like I just did back at your party. I've worked so hard since I graduated. I just want to ... *enjoy* myself for once."

"Of course. That's understandable."

"I meant to ask. Do you really think of me as a 'Mr. Straight'?"

"I do," says Willow. "I hope you're not offended."

"Not particularly," he said. "I suppose I've been called much worse."

Not knowing what else to say, Willow says, "I want to thank you for fixing my recumbent. How much do I owe? I'm a little low in cash, at the moment, just because ..."

Mr. Straight laughs. "*Owe* me? *You owe me nothing!* I almost killed you because my map was blocking my view for no reason at all—"

Willow nervously picks at her chocolate lava cake. Willow and Skip are the only two left inside the restaurant. The walls are sponge-painted a modern, metallic agave.

To Willow, this feels like her first *real* date since she graduated college.

What adults do ...

Remarkably exciting!

"This all reminds me of that scene in *Family Ties* when Mallory goes to the fancy restaurant with Nick!" Willow says. "You know, when Nick needs CPR but the only one who can perform it is the French waiter but he does it all wrong and he doesn't even speak English. Nick dies. It was so *funny*!"

Mr. Straight looks confused. "I'm sorry. We didn't have a television growing up."   *very rare for even back then*

Did Willow just hear correctly?

"You guys didn't have a TV?"

How is that even possible? Willow's family had six! Even one in the garage.

"We didn't. My parents never believed in pop culture. So ... I'm playing catch up now."

Could one ever possibly catch up? Willow isn't sure. Her brain is packed with treasured TV knowl-

159

edge, such as the reason for the death of Captain Stubing's fourth wife ("asphyxiation on the Lido deck due to overindulgence of Pina Coladas after passing out in the children's pool and then being strangled by Gopher"), the name of Bobby Brady's first pet guinea pig ("Manson"), and why the original Darrin was written off *Bewitched* (because he was turned into a flamingo by his witch mother-in-law and then run over with the sit-down mower operated by a very drunk Paul Lynde, off set).

Willow can't imagine *not* knowing this information. But, then again, Kevin works in *Business* and *Commerce*, and his Pop Culture IQ might not be so high ...

"Should we get the check?" he asks. There's a slight break in his voice.

Could he possibly be nervous?

Mr. Straight calls over for the waiter, the one with the fetlock of a greased ponytail. The one in the creased khakis and Y-back red suspenders, the latest, hottest fashion trend.

"Can I ... *help*?" asks Willow. "With the ... check?"

The waiter rolls his eyes.

Yet another female dressed as descended testicles after a safe-sex party pretending she's about to pick up the check.

"No," says Mr. Straight, smiling. "This one's on me."

"A sixth round of coffee?" asks the waiter.

"Why not," says Mr. Straight. "It is *Seattle*, after all."

Later, after Mr. Straight shakily pulls up to Willow's apartment building, after Mr. Straight removes the fixed recumbent bike from his BMW's trunk and hands it over, after Mr. Straight points out his new bumper sticker to Willow ("I didn't understand this but I know you love bumper stickers and this type of comedy!"), after Mr. Straight plants a warm kiss straight on Willow's receptive lips, after Mr. Straight is led upstairs, after Willow secretly places the mixed tape from out of her purse and into a far-away, most distant drawer, after Willow recounts her dinner in nuanced detail to Vicky ("blackened fish of some kind or another," "the chocolate lava cake practically exploded in my mouth!"), after Mr. Straight defecates from too much coffee, Willow and Mr. Straight retreat back into her bedroom and they make love.

It's certainly different than sleeping with Toody!

With Mr. Straight, there is *actual* foreplay!

When Mr. Straight orgasms, he does not scream through a distortion box about "fractured hearts!" or "melancholy rainbows!"

There is no strobe light to make Mr. Straight's face appear magical during orgasms!

There is nobody holding up a lighter and announcing that he just might have one "encore" left in him yet!

Willow wishes she had turned on her Fuji DS-100 digicam with 3-power zoom and shot for the four minutes!

But her documentary isn't about her sex life.

Who would be interested in that anyway?

It's really more about her friends and how they are *changing* the universe.

Three miles away, the safe sex party at Number One Vinyl Xperience has finally wound down and the secondary sex characteristics and STDs are leaving for the evening. A herpes simplex two sore vomits against the side of the building. A herpes simplex one sore watches.

In the parking lot, the Lost Boys are talking all things DC vs. Marvel.

"I prefer gods who want to be human rather than humans who wish to be gods," says Wes, from the rooftop. He's sipping a knock-off Icee-type drink from the (In)Convenience Mart called an "Eye Sea."

"What the hell does that mean?" says Spooner, rollerblading past and shooting a puck made out of Tower Record plastic bags into a makeshift net fashioned from out of medication bottles stolen from the failing pet store in the strip mall.

In Spooner's messenger's bag today is a very large check from the mayor to a children's cancer charity of some sort. Spooner has long since forgotten how long it's been in there.

"It means we're no different from the X-men," says Cody. "We're just *regular* people with superhuman abilities who are *loathed* by society."

Comfortably out of their Safe Sex outfits now and back into their Gen X outfits, the Lost Boys can talk more freely without any annoying inhibitions.

"Because we're too powerful," says Bake, next to

Wake, both relaxing against the brick wall.

"What's *your* superhuman ability?" asks Wes, from the roof.

"*Punching* the shit out of hypocrisy," says Bake, making a karate chop and kung fu noises and mistakenly waking Wake.

"How about yours?" asks Wes, pointing to Topper. "What's yours? Your superhuman ability?"

"Flying above the turbulence of everyday boomer bullshit."

"Mine is reading people's minds," says Bake.

Wake taps his forefinger against his head once to signify, *yes*, he agrees.

"Okay then, what am I thinking now?" asks Cody, making an exaggerated "thinking face" from within his iron lung. Graffitied across the iron lung is "*Avoid risk and rapid change!!*"

Bake scrunches his face as if in pain. "Dude, I don't even want to say out loud, it's so damned crazy. No, I will *not* suck your cock at the top of the Space Needle!"

"I wouldn't even suck your cock if it was the *last* cock on earth," says Wes.

"I wouldn't even suck your cock if it was on *fire*," says Bake.

"I wouldn't even suck your cock if it belonged to Demi Moore," says Cody.

"How about Miss Doubtfire?" says Spooner.

"Shit, I'd suck that *anyway*!" says Wes. "And yes."

"How much realistically," says Jack Jack. "How much realistically for any of you to take off all your clothes and run straight into the video store?"

"Ten bucks," says Spooner.

"Five," says Wes.

would rather talk about stuff then actually do it.

"I'd do it for free," says Jack Jack.

"Then *do* it," says Spooner.

"Can't," says Jack Jack. "*Busy.*"

"*Carpe diem*," says Wes, from the roof.

"What does that mean?" asks Jack Jack.

"Seize the day."

"And what's the opposite of that?"

"In Latin?"

"Yeah."

"Not sure. I'll find out tomorrow. If I *feel* like it."

It is Wes who first notices a stretch limousine pulling into the parking lot.

"Um, boys," he says. "Something important is happening."

"Well look at *that*," says Topper. "Our very own Tony Stark has just arrived."

"Billionaire Iron Man," says Wes. "Now I'd suck *that* iron dick."

"No, I'm serious," says Topper. "Our very *own* Tony Stark."

"And I'm *serious* too!" insists Wes.

A long stretch limousine (white) slows to a crawl and triple parks next to the record store. The motor stays on.

From out of a rear car door exits a man in stone-washed JNCO jeans, a super-tight choker leather necklace and a stud earring in his left ear.

He's holding a cherry wood cane with a gold eagle

164

on the tip.

He smells of rich.

It's Brendan Bryant, the inventor of the world's most killer hacky sack.

"Gentlemen," the man says. He tips his derby hat. "Had a *feeling* you might still be here. And you *are*."

"As I live and breathe," says Cody. "Brendan Bryant himself!"

"Looks like you don't even do that anymore," says Brendan Bryant. "Breathe."

Cody laughs. "Well, I am living. Just too lazy to breathe."

"God, it seems like *forever* ago," says Brendan Bryant. "*This* place. *Incredible*! The lot. Hasn't changed! At *all*!"

"When were you here last?" asks Wes.

Brendan looks different to Wes. More mature. Worldly. Also, he's never seen him from the vantage point of twelve-feet up.

"Six months ago," says Brendan Bryant. "And what are you doing up there? Why on a roof?"

"Gay," explains Royce. "Wes is gay. And we're all cool with that. You have a problem with that, fella?"

"Yes, I know," says Brendan Bryant. "No, I don't have a problem with it. But why on a roof?"

"Came out to his parents. Didn't go well," continues Royce. "Staying up there until they arrive to apologize."

"And if they don't?"

"Then he ain't coming down. It's our protest against homophobia."

"You think it'll be effective?" asks Brendan Bryant.

"How could it *not* be?" asks Bake from the wall.

"Hello, Bake. Haven't seen you in awhile. And hello, Wake. Still not talking?" asks Brendan.

"He's not," says Bake. "You here for the hacky-sack convention? Keynote speaker?"

"Tomorrow."

"Then back to San Francisco?" asks Bake from the wall.

"Palo Alto," says Brendan Bryant.

"Fuck is Palo Alto?" asks Topper, skateboarding past.

"North of San Francisco."

"Never heard of it," says Wes.

"But no," says Brendan Bryant. "Thinking I might just stick around after for a few days. There are so many opportunities."

Wes looks over to Topper. They both laugh.

"Opportunities? Like what? Selling umbrellas?" asks Wes.

"Oh, more than that," says Brendan Bryant. "An entire universe of possibility."

"I'll believe *that* when I see it," says Topper, rolling his eyes.

"Manna in heaven!" Brendan Bryant says suddenly, shaking his head. "All my friends from high school! *Look* at you guys!"

"Here we are," says Topper.

"How did you do it?" Royce asks, woozily.

Royce has just returned from a non-sanctioned medical experiment to earn enough money to buy

166

convenience mart roller dogs. He doesn't look so hot.

"Do *what*?"

"*Make* it," Royce says weakly. His left eye is fluttering. "Become *successful*."

"Had the idea for the perfect hacky sack. South African colors. New flag. Thought of it. Created the infomercial. Sold it."

"Yeah, but … *how*?"

Brendan Bryant looks off into the distance. "Do you see that, guys? I can see it. Can *you*?"

Wes, from the roof, narrows his eyes. "See *what*?"

"Yeah, *see* what?" asks Spooner, rollerblading past. "You talking about Jack Jack humping the ATM again?"

"No. *Beyond* that."

"Herpes simplex one fucking herpes simplex two behind a Dumpster?"

"No, even beyond *that*. You really can't see it?"

Wes shakes his head no.

As does Bake, as does Wake, who taps his forehead twice for no.

Royce doesn't make a move. A head shake just ain't in him tonight.

"The *world*. It's out there. And you're still … here. In a parking lot. Next to a failing convenience store, record store, and video store. A triumvirate of failure. An axis of losership."

In the distance, a foghorn can be heard. It's almost as if the director of this film never once visited Seattle.

"You go off and invent the perfect hacky sack, in the perfect South African colors, on a late-night infomercial, and you come back and talk to us like this?" asks Cody. He stops until his iron lung takes care of his next breath.

Then he finishes: "Is that what you're doing?"

"Fuck the hacky sack. Fuck *infomercials*. Can't you even conceive of what's out there?" Brendan is worked up now. "I mean, Cody, *look* at you! You want to work in a video store the rest of your life? *Skip.* Does Skip even know what music will be like in 2005? I don't. But it won't involve chasing after a customer after he buys a Toto CD. And *you*, Wes. You think you'll be alone, sitting on a roof forever?"

"Not if my parents apologize."

"Come with me, guys. When I leave in a few days. *Please.*"

"To Palo Alto?" asks Bake.

"Yes," says Brendan Bryant, tiredly. "To Palo Alto. Plenty of room in the limo."

"You got a jacuzzi in there?" asks Spooner, roller-blading past. "In that biggity, boppity, stretchity-assity limo-*zeeeeeeeeeeeen* of youze?!"

"What do you want out of life, Spooner?" asks Brendan Bryant. "Rollerblading champion of Seattle still?"

"What's wrong with that?" asks Spooner. "I *can* do it! And I *will*!"

"What does that even mean?" asks Brendan Bryant. "Come with me."

"We like it here," says Bake.

"We do," says Wes. "We really *do* like it here."

"You got a TV in there?" asks Spooner, roller-

168

blading past again. "In that big ol' vehicle of yours?"

Topper skateboards over to Brendan. "Bring it in, bro." He hugs Brendan Bryant. "I missed you, bruv."

"I missed you guys, too. I *really* have!"

Wake walks over and silently inspects the limo. He runs his hands along the smooth lines. He peaks into the driver's side window but it's darkened. The engine remains on.

"Come with me," says Brendan Bryant, one last time.

"How much realistically?" says Spooner. "To take this bad boy through a McDonald's drive-through and order just one French fry?"

"How much realistically," says Topper. "To stop at a stoplight and then ask to drag the car next to you?"

"How much realistically," says Jack Jack. "To put a bumper sticker on the back that says MY OTHER CAR IS ALSO A RENTED STRETCH LIMOUSINE?"

"I'd do it for free," says Cody.

"One problem," says Bake. "You don't own a car. Let alone a limo."

Cody shrugs.

S.W.A.S.

Sealed. With. A.

Shrug.

"Guys, it was great seeing you again," says Brendan Bryant, with a tip of his hat and a tap of his cane. "You all look … " He pauses, trying to think of just the right *word*. They all wait anxiously to see what he comes up with.

"You all *look*."

"Thanks!" says Jack Jack.

"I wish you all the best. I *do* miss you. Keep in touch."

"We don't write letters," says Bake. "Just use the pay phone."

"That may be changing," says Brendan Bryant. "Imagine a pay phone through a typewriter. Or a computer. Being able to communicate that way. Well, it's *happening*."

"Say *whaaaaaaa*?" asks Wes from the roof. "You talking the goofy goof?"

All laugh. The Lost Boys, anyway.

"It's not the silly talk," says Brendan, patiently. "And, for the record, this limousine is mine. It's not rented."

The driver's side window slides down. A woman sticks her head out. She is beautiful.

Cody whistles.

"Jessica," says Brendan Bryant. "Jessica: my driver and assistant. These are the Lost Boys. We went to high school together. And hung for awhile. Right here in this ol' parking lot."

"I know about fifteen Jessicas," says Wes.

"Not like *this* Jessica, you don't," says Cody, making a motion for his iron lung to be pushed closer.

"Now why would anyone this beautiful hang around our Brendan?" asks Spooner. "No one did back when we were in school!"

Topper pushes Cody's iron lung closer. Cody takes a deep and involved sniff. It's been a long while since he's flirted with a live woman.

"Girl, I *smell* ya," he says.

Jessica winces.

It appears, sadly, that the female species still aren't all too keen on men in iron lungs ... even if they do wear ironic T-shirts.

"Are you the assistant we talked with on the pay phone?" Jack Jack asks.

Jessica laughs. "Are you the one who asked me to define irony?"

"Must have been Royce," says Cody. "He's *always* asking that!"

"I see," says Jessica.

She doesn't appear to care. She's too gorgeous. Brendan Bryant enters the car, closes the door, and without so much as a fancy beep of the horn, the limousine takes off and then out of the parking lot.

To break the uncomfortable silence, Wes speaks up.

"New topic," he says from the roof. "Mr. Furley versus Mr. Roper. Who was the funnier one?"

The boys perk up.

"*Come and knock on my door*!" sings Bake.

Wake dances along.

"*Someone's waiting for you ...*"

"Mr. Furley! No competition!" says Cody. "Not even close!"

"Better topic," says Cody. "The first or *second* Chrissy."

"There was only *one* Chrissy," says Bake. "The other blonde chick was Chrissy's *sister*, Cindy."

"She was his *cousin*, you asshole," says Topper, skateboarding over to the Convenience Mart. A new customer has just arrived, a regular for his Zig Zags. "She was his *cousin*. Not her *sister*. She was from a farm and clumsy as *shit*."

Things are back to normal for the Lost Boys. So many important topics are discussed throughout the night.

And by the time the sun rises over the parking lot, and by the time Royce heads off to another unsanctioned medical experiment, this one involving ketamine to pay for Convenience Store dried jerky, and by the time Skip arrives to open the store with Toby the Wonder Dog along in tow (dressed this morning as the little-known brain-damaged Sweathog, Bennie), the Lost Boys have come to the conclusion that Mr. Roper was most definitely the funnier landlord and that Chrissy was absolutely, without question, more beautiful than Cindy, her cousin.

Not even close.

It has been a *colossal* evening.

Saturday, 1:15 P.M.

"I hear Toody is none too thrilled," says Vicky, walking beside Willow. The pace is slow. Vicky is wearing her super thick club-foot corrective shoes, the latest fashion trend.

"Let him be," Willow says, neck hickeys all fresh and moist, glistening. "Mr. Straight ain't so *straight* in bed. *Wow*!"

"You sounded like two feral creatures going at it," says Vicky, in mock horror. "I'm so *mad* that I had to hear that!"

But Vicky isn't really and truly mad.

See, for people of Vicky's and Willow's generation, listening to others having sex ain't no big "thang."

"Hope we didn't disturb you," says Willow, sarcastically and faux embarrassed. "Tried to drown it out with loud music. Guess it didn't work."

She was wrong that "Touch Me I'm Sick" played loud enough would ever drown out the primeval jungle noises.

No prob. She'll just have to turn it up *louder* next time—that is, if Mr. Straight will allow her. He'd probably prefer "In the Air Tonight" or "The Jellicle Ball" from *Cats*, but that's okay. Great relationships consist of musical compromise.

Besides, who is she to question someone who works in Commerce?

"How did Toody even know?" Willow asks. "And why would he even care? I'm just assuming he slept with the Syphilitic Sore."

"Words gets around fast when people move slow," says Vicky, wisely. "Where's Mr. Straight now?"

"Had an important business meeting this morning."

"He left early?"

"He did."

"How far is this video dating place?"

"Couple blocks."

"Vicky, can I get serious here?"

"Sure."

"I am nothing with you," Willow says earnestly.

Vicky laughs. She knows this game.

"A good friend isn't hard to find," Willow says in return.

"From the moment I met you," Vicky declares, smiling, "I knew you wouldn't change my life."

"Friendship is the most precious gift in the world," says Willow, also smiling. "Not counting money."

"Friendship is the best thing money can buy."

"With you, I'm half the woman that I am alone."

"Without you, I'd achieve the entirety of my dreams."

Both laugh very hard. It's an old game for them. They've been playing for more than a week now.

"I'm tired," declares Vicky, suddenly. She stops walking. She has no time for such physical activity. She immediately sticks out a thumb … as well as one of her super thick corrective shoes in a most coquett-ish manner. The ruse works. *too lazy to even walk*

174

A car immediately pulls over to the side of the road.

A red 1984 Pontiac Grand Am.

Looks *familiar*.

Both girls run towards it. But stop.

It's Skip.

Jesus hell. Of course! Willow should have recognized the "INSERT FUNNY SAYING HERE" bumper sticker.

"Ladies," says Skip from out of the open window. His cassette player is blasting "Revolution Come and Gone" by Beat Happening, a group he feels is 100% better than either the Rolling Stones or the Who— even combined. "Hop your lil' grunge selves in!"

Vicky looks at Willow. *Should they? It is nice to walk once a month or so. And it is their day off. Then again, they do have an awfully long distance to travel—at least a quarter mile.*

Willow shrugs. They climb into the backseat, if a bit reluctantly.

"Couldn't keep away from me," Skip says, smiling.

"I guess not," says Willow. "Where you headed? Why aren't you in the store?"

"Have something to take care of," says Skip.

"Who's minding the shop?" Willow asks.

"Toby," says Skip. "Dressed as Ed Asner from *Mary Tyler Moore*. No one will cross him. Hello, Vicky! How are you?"

"Ahoy there, cap'n," says Vicky. "Caught between the devil and the deep blue sea."

"Where you girls headed? To the yeast infection aisle to dance the Safety Dance?"

"Not today," says Willow. "Vicky's going to check out the eligible men at SEATTLE VIDEO DATING SERVICES!"

Vicky punches Willow in the arm. "Thanks, jack-ass! Embarrassing enough!"

"What are you looking for exactly?" asks Skip, ejecting the CD and putting on 88.3, the 10-watt FM mono pirate station rumored to be broadcasting from out of a shrimp boat on Elliott Bay.

A rich voice, that of DJ Truth, is heard:

"I'm right here, folks. I got my bottle of Orbitz, complete with the swirling flavor bubbles, I got my stick of Fruit Stripe, I got my microphone, I got crazy ways, people. I got my freedom, brothers! But do you know what I don't have? Thanks for asking and I shall now tell you: I don't have love. What does it take in this city to find real love? How far should one go? Not in miles. But in loneliness? Can I hold out? Should anyone ever hold out for something so necessary?"

"*That's* who I want," says Vicky, from the back-seat. "DJ Truth. Take me to him right now!"

"He doesn't record live," says Skip. "It's all taped."

"And you would know that how?" asks Willow.

"Because we are acquainted," says Skip. "Haven't talked in years but I know him."

Vicky sits forward. "You *know* DJ Truth?"

"Of course," says Skip. "We grew up together. His brother knew mine. We all went to Franklin.

176

Class of '82."

"Which would make you ... eighty-three?" asks Willow.

"Twenty-nine," answers Skip. "And feeling *great*. I mean, *fine*. Feeling great was twenty-*eight*. 'Eating at 7-Eleven' was twenty-*seven*. You *don't* want to meet this guy, Vicky. He's a wild one. *Trust* me."

"What's his real name?"

"Can't tell you."

"I could just look in the yearbook for him."

"And what would you be looking for exactly?"

"Where are you taking us, Skip?" asks Willow. "This is the opposite direction of the video-dating place, Realistic Expectations."

Willow is still tired—and, truth be told, a bit *sore*—from last night.

"I'm taking the Vickster home."

"The Vickulator," says Vicky.

"The Vickerator," says Willow. "The Vicker*nator*!"

"Vicky who like da dicky!" says Vicky.

Both Willow and Vicky collapse into giggles.

"Not taking Vicky to that stupid video dating service. She deserves *better*," says Skip. "But I am taking you, Willow, to this meeting."

Willow isn't happy. Vicky, on the other hand, is relieved. She wasn't into this video dating thing anyway. She can now just head straight home to check out the latest issue of *Sassy* and masturbate to the photo spread of Rick Moranis.

A song comes on the radio.

It is one of DJ Truth's absolute favorites.

Skip sings along. Apparently, it's also one of his favorites.

It's called "All Out!"

All out! Out pop songs!
Out lame mainstream movies!
Jazzercise, tanning booths, silicon boobies!
Out nuclear bombs! Out nuclear war!
My head is fucked up and it's gettin' all sore!
I. Just want. All out!

Out yuppies!
Out golfing!
Out suburban sprawl!
Makes me want to shoot myself at the mall!
Out ranch style houses!
Out lame family values!
I broke into your country club just to say
"screw you!"
I. Just want. All out!

Infomercials, talk show wars, parental
advisory!
I don't even want my dang MTV!
Politics in Washington! Budget for defense!
Come on people! Can't we just use some
common sense?

Isn't it ironic to keep shopping at the Gap?!
I just spilled a Starbucks all over my lap!
I. Just want it. All out!

I. Just want it. All out!
I. Just want it. All out! ...

The car comes to a stop outside Willow and Vicky's apartment building.

As does the song.

"Hey, Vicky!" Willow yells after her. "Just give the video dating thing a chance, huh? Maybe some time down the road?"

Vicky shrugs and exits the car. "Fuck chance."

"Now do you want to tell me why we're here?" Willow asks Skip, as they pull away.

"Meeting," Skip says, fiddling with the radio dial.

"Okay," says Willow. "Any more information, Yoda?"

"I am the owner of the Number One Vinyl Xperience store," declares Skip.

"No shit," says Willow. "And I am the employee of the Number One Vinyl Xperience store."

"Yes. But I am *not* the *owner* of the *strip mall* in which the Number One Vinyl Xperience store *resides*."

"And who might that be?"

"Well, the previous owner, as of yesterday, was a nice man who didn't at all mind that the store didn't make any money. Or that a group of misfits was living in his parking lot. He just doesn't—*or didn't*—seem to mind."

"He sounds cool. Like your average landlord."

"Yes. But Seattle is changing. Ever since that damn video—"

"Both Vicky and I arrived *before* 'Smells Like Spirit' aired!" Willow screams.

How many damn times does she have to tell him?!

"I know, I know!" says Skip, twisting the radio knob. "That's not the issue. The issue here is there's now a new owner of the strip mall. I received a call this morning. And he wants to meet in person to discuss some issues."

"And who might this be?"

"He didn't say."

"And I'm here to provide support? I'm tired and … a little sore."

"From the car accident?"

"Um, yes."

"What?"

"*Yes!*"

Skip pulls in front of a downtown business building and easily finds a space just out front.

"Toby can watch the store till we're back," says Skip. "I'm just happy to have run into you. Not exactly a champ in social settings."

"You did okay at the Safe Sex party," Willow says, as they exit the car and make their way to the entrance.

The building looks familiar but Willow can't *quite* place it.

"Maybe. But if I did, it didn't hurt that I was wearing pubic-crab mincers and Ping Pong balls cut in half for eyes."

"That *does* tend to help ones chances," Willow admits, entering the lobby. "I thought you looked great."

"If I could only work up the nerve to ask out Vicky," says Skip, pocketing his keys.

"Then why don't you? Just ask her out already, would you? Pull the damn ripcord!"

"I'm not her type. She seems like the DJ Truth type."

"Vicky likes DJ Truth because he states his feelings like a *man*. Like an *adult*. You should do the *same*, Skip."

"Top five songs about not adequately expressing your feelings as an adult. Starting at the very top: Talk Talk's 'Eden' off their gorgeous 1988 masterpiece *Spirit of Eden* ..."

Willow rolls her eyes. They enter the elevator and Skip presses the button for the eleventh floor.

This all seems very similar, she thinks. *Did I dream about this place? There's just something so* familiar *about it!*

All of it.

The elevator stops at the eleventh floor and the doors open wide.

And then Willow knows at once that she did *not* dream this.

This is Mr. Straight's office! It's only been three days but it feels like a lifetime ... or a movie written by a writer who's never experienced real life.

"Oh my god," whispers Willow to Skip. "I've *been* here."

"When?"

"Three days ago."

"Are you joking?"

181

Even though he's a fictional character, it's tough for Skip to believe that Willow couldn't possibly have not remembered something so simple.

"No. It didn't even occur to me until we just stepped off the elevator that this *must* be the place! This place of Business. Of Commerce. Where … they create … *finance*."

The secretary is there to welcome them. "May I help you?" she asks officiously.

"I already know where to go," says Willow, remembering the way to Mr. Straight's all-glass and lucite office.

"Why were you here to begin with?" asks Skip, looking around nervously. "This isn't your world."

"Mr. Straight works here," Willow mumbles.

"Oh no."

"Which means …"

"Which means we have a new boss. And that boss's name is—"

"Mr. Straight," finishes Skip.

They walk past a paper plate with cake crumbs and a dirty white plastic knife still sitting on the kitchen counter. A stuffed Dilbert doll hangs inside one cubicle with a handwritten dialogue balloon stapled to it: "*i'myay osay iredtay ofyay work!*"

Pig latin for "I'm so tired of work!"

This place ain't fucking around.

By the time they reach the exquisite office, Mr. Straight is standing, waiting, leaning against his lucite desk. He seems surprised to see Willow. He reaches out to shake Skip's hand, who refuses.

182

"Skip, I'm so *happy* you could make it."

"Kevin, what's happening?" asks Willow.

"Have a seat," says Mr. Straight. "*Please*." He motions to two very modern chairs on rollers.

"I think we can stand," says Willow, not moving. Chairs on wheels have always made her very nervous. "We do it all day in the office—*stand*."

"That's true," says Mr. Straight. "It's the one advantage you have over me and the rest of us losers who have to sit in front of a computer all day!"

He laughs heartily but neither Willow or Skip join in.

"Is this the meeting you rushed out for this morning?" Willow asks Mr. Straight.

"Yes," says Mr. Straight. "I wasn't expecting you to join. If I knew, I could have just driven you over myself."

"So I suppose you're the new owner of the strip mall?" Skip asks, already knowing the answer.

"I am," says Mr. Straight. "And of your store."

"I own my store."

"Not anymore. New landlord. *Me*."

Skip looks to Willow. *Could this really be happening?*

"And I suppose you're going to kick me out?" Skip finally manages to get out.

"Not at all," Mr. Straight says.

"Kevin, is this your *business*?" Willow asks. "*Buying strip-malls*?"

"No," says Mr. Straight. "My business would be taking over failing businesses and *improving* them."

183

"And *how* do you intend to do that with my store?" asks Skip, looking as if he might need to take a seat after all, wheels or no wheels.

"By … gently suggesting that we modernize. That we leap into 1992. And not chase customers out who might want Aerosmith on 'inferior' compact discs. They're here to stay, Skip. We're going to learn that. *Together*."

"You are something," says Skip. "Truly *something*."

Willow has only seen Skip this angry once before—when a customer mocked Toby the Wonder Dog because he was dressed as Maude from the infamous abortion episode.

"Possibly," says Mr. Straight. "But that's Business."

"The Convenience Mart? And video store, too?" Willow asks, feeling woozy.

"Yes, *those* too!" Mr. Straight looks at both Willow and Skip. "You're both acting like this isn't a *good* thing. It *is*! There's more money to be made for *everyone*!"

Willow can't help but think:

Now where will Wes uselessly protest homophobia?

Now where will Spooner train for the Seattle rollerblading championship, whatever the hell that is, if it even exists, which it probably doesn't?

Now where will Cody wear a hobo's hat and eat a microwavable shit pizza and not *be threatened with arrest?*

184

It's all so damn sad!

"Capitalism," says Skip.

"*Capitalism*," repeats Mr. Straight. "Yes. Don't you love it? *Capitalism*."

He draws out the final word, savors it, as one would the precious last swallow from a freshly-popped bottle of Zima. Mr. Straight once read that "Zima" means "winter" in Slavic languages. He can definitely understand why.

God, how he longs for one now.

"It's people like you who are ruining this city," says Skip, barely holding back tears. It's the first time he actually might weep since the 1988 Talking Heads album *Naked* failed to make number one. "You take what makes this city so unique and you turn it into a commercialized *zero zone* for the masses!"

"No hard feelings, Skip. It's only—"

"Business?" Skip snarls sarcastically.

"Yes," says Mr. Straight. "Business."

"Is that why you came into the store for the first time?" asks Willow. "To see if it was even worth buying?"

"It was," says Mr. Straight.

"And is that why you hit my recumbent with your car?" she asks.

"No!" says Mr. Straight, laughing. "That would make me a sociopath! That was an *honest* hit. I was just trying to read a map. They're very cumbersome. Especially when obstructing my view when I'm driving to work on the same route I take each and every day."

"I finally thought I had found a good one," says Willow, shaking her head. "Finally found a good man. I mean, we didn't meet in the traditional way, like, say, after I was put in charge of making sure the laxatives forced down your throat did their job, but it was still *cute*, right?"

Mr. Straight looks confused.

"Read over the contract," he finally states, handing it over to Willow, who only reluctantly accepts. "*Please.* This is for the best. You'll see. Would you like one of the yummy donuts Marcy brought, even though it's not Wednesday?"

What is it with people who work in offices and who love their donuts? And plastic knives with globs of cake icing, sitting forlornly in kitchens?

Skip grabs the contract out of Willow's hand and begins to read aloud.

"Number one: no making lists," he says. "Number two …"

Willow grabs it back.

"No gum chewing," reads Willow.

They put their heads together.

"No dogs dressed as TV characters," says Skip.

"No holding Safe Sex parties with customers dressed as secondary—or even *first*—sex characteristics," says Willow.

"No mocking fans of Aerosmith or Rush or Kansas." Skip pauses and rubs his eyes. "Jesus. Dust in my fucking *asshole*."

"No lice at the listening station?!" asks Willow, incredulous.

"This is *outrageous*," announces Skip, squeezing the contract. "*Inhuman! Nazi* like!"

"What I'm proposing is not unreasonable," says Mr. Straight. "The city is changing and so is the world. Let's improve the store with an *upgrade*! To *all* the stores! Make 'em modern and lively and kicky and *fun*!"

"I like my store the way it is," says Skip.

"I'm afraid it's no longer your store to run," says Mr. Straight.

"I can't even work in my own store?"

"Willow will become the manager of the record store. As for you, you're free to work *anywhere*."

"And what exactly is my role here?" Skip asks quietly.

"I don't know. *Assistant* manager?"

Skip reddens. "This is *my* store. That I built! And ran into the ground! And you now have the temerity to tell me that I'm *assistant* manager?"

Skip has never used the word "temerity" before. He heard it the previous week on a *Nightline* segment about the inherent dangers of *Beavis and Butthead* and he's been itching to try it ever since.

He *likes* it.

"Shit, I don't care!" says Mr. Straight. "Hell, make that dog—what's he called?"

"Toby the Wonder Dog," mutters Skip.

"Make Toby the Wonder Dog the goddamn assistant manager! Skip, you're free to open a failing record store anywhere you please. Just not here. May I ask you something?"

Mr. Straight waits for an answer from Skip that doesn't seem to be arriving. He continues:

"Just a quick question: When did it all begin to go wrong? Your life and stuff?"

"You bastard," says Skip.

"Been called worse."

"So how long do we have?" asks Skip, curtly.

"Tomorrow at 10:00 AM, when the new store opens," says Mr. Straight. "Willow, I'll see you later tonight?"

Willow can only look at him in absolute wonder. *Is this freak for real?*

"This is just business," Mr. Straight declares. "This is how the *real* world works. Outside of the parking lot and those failing stores."

Willow says nothing.

"I'll call you, Willow," he says, smiling and standing. The meeting is over. He goes to hug Willow, who recoils. "That's okay. But I think I left my condom tie at your place."

"Does your heart die when you go into business?" Willow asks.

"Only if you want it to," says Mr. Straight, going in for another hug.

She recoils again.

"I *never* want it to," says Willow. "You fooled me, Kevin. I thought you were decent. Even if you were a straight."

Mr. Straight returns to his lucite desk and shrugs. With a wave of his hand, he sends Willow and Skip out and returns to the small device that holds five metal balls hanging from wires.

Willow can hear the *clicky-clack* on her way out.

It's almost like something from out of a movie.

"Top five songs having to do with assholes," says Skip on the way to the elevator. "'Something That You Said' by the Beautiful South ...'"

On her way out, Willow grabs a donut. *Why not, right? If Mr. Straight doesn't want to play fair, why should she?*

Willow grabs a fistful of pens.

And a batch of pencils.

And a box of erasers.

And a sheaf of dot-matrix printing papers ...

And a bag of paper clips.

And the cake-crusty plastic knife.

Also, the stuffed Dilbert doll.

onglay aymay eway uckfay ommercialismcay!

"Long may we fuck commercialism!"

Long live Anarchy!

STEWART

Pros
- HOT
- free weed
- good sense of style
- in a band!!

Cons
- pretty sure he likes Sara ??
- weird ear lobes
- his friends are dicks
- is a scorpio ☹

189

Saturday, 4:25 P.M.

"You did *what*?" asks Wes from the roof.

Willow removes the lens cap from her Fuji DS-100 digicam with 3-power zoom. She hits the red POWER button and begins to film.

"Stole some pens." *capitalism considered bad then*

"Badass, anti-commerce gesture!" announces Bake from the wall. He returns to sipping his juice box of Ssips.

"Also some *paper clips*," brags Willow.

God knows what she'll do with any of these office supplies but still ...

"That's fantastic!" said Topper skateboarding past, grabbing the plastic knife from out of Willow's hand and giving it a big ol' sniff. "Dude tried to get me to come down to his office earlier and I refused. He called the pay phone. I ain't selling."

He drops the knife.

"I'm afraid it's too late," says Willow. "Mr. Straight now owns this entire parking lot. And all of the stores associated with it—our *entire world*."

"Ownership is nothing but a humanistic conceit," says Wes from the roof.

"A conceit of what?" Cody asks, sitting on the overturned trash can and wearing a T-shirt with Toucan Sam the Fruit Loops cereal mascot. On Toucan's beak, close to the tip, is white cocaine residue.

Cody is no longer within his iron lung. He found

190

it way too much effort getting from one side of the parking lot to the other.

"*Reality*," says Wes. "We've already been through this."

"Wonder if Mr. Straight is controlling the narrative here," says Spooner, rollerblading past. "Maybe he's now our god. And we're programmed by Mr. Straight to do whatever he wants."

"Well, if we *are* being programmed, I say that we all now give Mr. Straight the big middle finger!" screams Cody.

"I say we *do* it!" screams back Topper.

All of the Lost Boys flip their fingers to the brackish sky above.

It's a sight to behold.

"And … *perfect*!" says Willow, pressing "STOP". "You guys are going to be *world* famous!"

"Willow, you seem a lot happier than you should," says Topper. "Mr. Straight is now the owner of Skip's store."

"I'm fine," says Willow. "Skip's the mess."

"Where is he?" asks Bake.

"Inside the store. Re-organizing his records before he boxes them up to re-organize again at home."

"In what order this time?" asks Royce. He drops to the ground and flops around like the fish in Faith No More's "Epic" video.

The groups laughs.

They stop laughing. It's not a gag.

"In order of sadness," says Willow. "Have to get back to work. Someone pick up Royce. His scar's oozing. See you guys later."

Willow enters the store. The chimes that used to play "Burning Down the House" have been dismantled.

Willow sees Skip sitting in an aisle of the store, next to a pile of records. She approaches and sits beside him. She says nothing. Neither does he.

What can one say, really?

She thinks about turning the video camera on Skip and pressing RECORD but thinks otherwise. No use.

"What did you ever see in the guy?" Skip eventually asks, loading LPs into a storage box. "Because you fell for him. *Hard.* What exactly was the problem with Toody? Besides him performing karate moves whenever sexually stimulated? And having an ear plug jammed up his nose?"

"I guess ... I just wanted someone ... *adult*," Willow says. "Someone who apologized after he farted."

"Well, you sure found him," says Skip. "And I hope you're real happy with your apologizer of farts now."

"I'm sorry, Skip," says Willow. "I really am."

Toby the Wonder Dog approaches and whimpers. He's not in costume today.

Skip just wasn't in the mood to think of one.

It occurs to Willow that this Temple to Alternativeness, this record store, shall be no longer.

With its metal H.R. Pufnstuf lunch box by the register.

With its Johnny Rotten clock, two punk legs measuring out the workday's hours and minutes.

192

With its hilarious sign over the bathroom that reads DISASTER AREA!

Gone.

Nightmare!

It is an American tragedy.

The Kennedy Assassination.

Vietnam.

Jonestown.

This.

"Did you ever think of doing anything else?" asks Willow. "I mean, do you *have* to own a record store in a failing strip mall?"

"What else am I going to do, Willow? Work in an office with ... *donuts*? And *computers*? And boxes of pens and *pencils*? This isn't *work* ... this ... this is my *life*. You don't have to keep working here, you know. There's a whole world out there. You don't have to stay."

"Where would I go?" Willow answers. "I've seen what commercialism has wrought."

Willow has never used the word "wrought" before, at least correctly. But she heard it the previous week on a *Nightline* segment about the moral implications of Murphy Brown conceiving a child, out of wedlock, inside a National Air & Space Smithsonian bathroom, and she's longed to use it ever since.

She likes it.

"And I have to finish my documentary on my generation," she continues. "If I don't ..." She pauses. There's a catch in her throat. "If I don't, then, well ... I don't know what my *purpose* is. I really don't. Oh,

Skip, I'm so *sorry*. I got waylaid by life ... "

Skip, not adept at physical contact, is slow to hug Willow, but when he does, it is genuine—if a tad bizarre and disturbing. It reminds Willow of a back-stage hug she once witnessed at the '92 H.O.R.D.E. Festival that involved Ben Folds and himself.

"Okay, okay," says Willow, eventually. "Come on." She stops crying and wipes her tear with one flanneled sleeve. "Come on, Skip. That's enough now. Seriously! I kinda prefer you when you're all grouchy. And we have a ton of *work* to do."

It's true.

There's a ton of work to accomplish.

"And so there is," says Skip sadly. "So many memories."

"Like what?" asks Willow.

"Just so many," answers Skip. "Um, a lot."

"Like what?" asks Willow. "Just one."

"Like... not selling Van Halen to that guy."

Willow nods.

That *is* a good memory.

Thinking back on it, they both get to work.

Meanwhile, on the other end of town, Vicky has decided—perhaps against her better judgment—to take Willow's advice and to maybe, *just maybe*, give this new video dating "thing" a shot.

It couldn't be any worse than hooking up with men behind '70s-themed pinball machines in seedy bars, right?

Actually, yes, it *could* be worse...

Vicky has now just finished her third date of the

194

afternoon.

So many awful, but funny dates!

There was the man who was perfect in all aspects, save for the sperm in his hair, which was not his.

There was the man with the S&M Dungeon, filled from top to bottom with boxed Ikea equipment. He desperately needed Vicky's help installing it. All of it. *"Do you hear, my bitch?!"*

Vicky didn't mind a little torture, but this was too much.

There was the man who blamed all of his life's failures and three divorces on the fact that his father went out for cigarettes one morning, back in 1976, and always came back.

Then there was the drummer for Candlebox.

No, the afternoon and evening has not gone well. By the time Vicky is finished, five hours after she's begun, by the time she's back in her room, no hair band needed tonight around the doorknob, her "old-timey" throwback plastic radio tuned into DJ Truth, by the time she's lying on her futon, or "screwton" as she likes to call it, by the time the clock strikes twelve, it is only then does it occur to her that there's only one man in Seattle who's perfect for her.

And he's now talking to her live—or on *tape*, if Skip is correct—from whatever location he happens to broadcast, whether it's on a shrimp boat on Elliott Bay or from the very top of the Seattle Space Needle.

Because, as always, DJ Truth is speaking the truth, loud and strong:

"I'm only talking to one person tonight," DJ Truth

says through a voice scrambler. *"I've been told she's a fan of what I say. I want her to know—and it is a she— I want her to know that she is not alone. She is surrounded by love and by friendship. I want her to know that she might now exist between two worlds, her childhood and her future, and it might very well be scary. She may use sex as a buffer between emotional pain and the feeling of oblivion. That all may be true. But what's also true is that I'm here for you ... if no one else. If nothing else, just please know that."* about

Vicky sits up. another movie came out about wise DJ. Pimp

Did she just hear correctly? up the volume

Or is she still high from the 'shrooms bought from an armless dude at last week's Air Sex contest?

No, this is really *happening!*

She reaches over for her cordless telephone and dials Willow's beeper. She waits for Willow's brief message and then presses the # sign and the numerals "414-582."

Similar to the language spoken and understood between twins, Vicky and Willy have invented a long list of words and phrases represented by beeper code that only *they* can comprehend.

Vicky waits for a response to "Emergency! Call!" It quickly arrives:

"39-811!" (*What's going on? Are you okay?!*)

"282-281!" (*Yes!*)

"2921-281!" (*So what's going on?*)

"2991-282" (*What?*)

"2921-281!!!!!" (*So what's going on!!!!!*)

"281038-181" (*Okay. Relax! I went out on a few*

196

dates this afternoon. They were terrible. But something ... interesting happened after.)

"21948-281" (*Sex disease?*)

"81817-282" (*No!*)

"281-8582" (*Joined the French Legion for the hot guys?*)

"29201-281" (*No! I did that once! Maybe I should just call?*)

"2991-282" (*What?*)

"7107-71" (*Call now please!*)

"2991-282" (*What?!*)

"3817-89" (*Just give me a goddamn call!!!!!*)

Within moments, Vicky's phone rings.

"Are you okay?" Willow asks. "Not chained to a Motel 6 bed?"

"Not this time," Vicky says. "This time I'm *more* than okay."

"Did you do the video dating like I asked?"

"I did."

"And?"

"Terrible."

"What happened?"

"Drummer. Candlebox."

"Oh, Vicky. That is so awful!"

"But something also *good* happened! Skip must have talked with his high school friend DJ Truth!"

"Skip is here with me now in the record store. He's pulling down all his Fugazi posters and shaking with rage. He promises to one day meet with Ian MacKaye and share a non-alcoholic beer—"

"DJ Truth just talked about me!"

"How do you know it was about you?"

"It *had* to be about me, Willow! I think I might have a chance!"

"Vicky, can we speak more about this when I next see you?"

"I guess. Why?"

"Because Royce just came into the store and is asking if we sell parakeets. He's very high. And I have a ton of !!HOT HOT HOT COMPACT DISCS!! signs to hang."

"Yes," says Vicky, smiling. She hasn't remembered the last time she smiled.

Maybe it was when she saw the editorial cartoon in the local alt weekly. It featured the Statue of Liberty giving a blow job to Uncle Sam.

Vicky forgets the editorial reason for the cartoon.

Maybe it was just that the Statue was horny for liberty.

"Grand opening here is tomorrow at ten, Vipster. I'll see you then."

Willow hangs up. So does Vicky.

Willow get back to work.

It is going to be a long night.

Sunday, 9:38 A.M.

It's been a *long* night.

The construction noises have kept Willow awake for the majority of it, even as she tried—perhaps a little bit naively—to catch a quick nap in what used to be the incense stick aisle, one of Toby's paws over her tummy, her own body leaning uncomfortably against Skip's old metal desk.

Most of the work had been done by a crew of blue-collars, each one wearing a pair of white overalls. If the Oompa Loompas had their own union and lived in the northwest and wore Patagonia and were not dwarves but quite tall and powerful and emanating the odor of tree sap and custody battles, these would be those guys.

They've since left.

Blisters in all the wrong places, thought Willow. *And for all the wrong reasons.*

The store's LPs have been packed away in cardboard boxes and taped shut, the life-size cardboard standout of a frowning Morrissey placed gently into the trunk of Skip's 1984 Pontiac Grand Am, the framed Paul Westerberg guitar pic from the Replacement's last-ever Seattle show lovingly dusted and inserted into its velvet-lined box in preparation for the day when the Rock and Roll Hall of Fame finally has the fucking *balls* to vote in the *good* bands.

It's now almost time for the store's grand

re-opening.

Skip takes a quick peak outside. The store is set to open at precisely 10:00 A.M.

"Hell of a line out there," he says, shaking his head.

Skip walks into his back office, now complete with a fancy oak desk.

And a brand-new Aeron chair.

With *wheels*.

And a map of the United States with each state's best-selling pop band highlighted with a brightly colored push-pin.

Willow follows him back. "They really did a number to our good ol' office, huh?"

Skip looks around. "Yeah. End of an era." *Sad*

"Skip, I feel that this is entirely my fault."

"Would have happened had you not dated him," says Skip. "Let's be honest."

"Possibly. But this doesn't make it any better."

"Willow, how long have you worked here now?"

"Six days?" she answers. "Seven?"

Willow can't remember. *Awhile.*

"Whatever it's been, it's been long enough to see that this city is changing."

"I arrived *before* the video," states Willow. "By *minutes*."

"I realize that," says Skip. "You're grandfathered. But the rest of this city, I don't know. It just seems … *emptier*. A mimeograph of what it used to be."

"A mimeograph?" asks Willow.

"A Xerox," says Skip, a bit dramatically. "Maybe I *am* getting old. My work here is done, Willow. I'm sorry. But you're on your own. C'mon, Toby."

"Where are you going?"

"Home," he says.

"Skip, please don't do anything drastic."

"Like *what*?" He laughs. "Like listening to an album with another person? That *sort* of drastic?"

"Just … *please*. Take *care* of yourself."

"Skip will be fine," Skip says. "Always has been, always will be. Good luck today. I'm sorry I can't be here to witness the store's transition. It's just … too *new Seattle*."

"Skip?"

"Bye, Willow."

"No list tonight?"

"You don't like them anyway."

"But I do!"

Skip smiles and shakes his head. He knows better.

He exits with Toby by his side. The dog looks particularly wretched without a costume, almost freakishly unnatural. Anything would be better. Even Toby dressed as Latka from *Taxi*.

Willow watches as the two leave the store, Toby's tail sandwiched between his legs, Skip carrying out yet another box of records, a pricing gun sticking out of his back pocket.

There they go, out the door.

New opening chords to a song Willow can't quite place can be heard. Not exactly jaunty.

Will price guns even be used in the future?

Willow takes a long look around the store.

What a different place from only yesterday!

201

No more haphazard records leading every which way but loose.

Just row upon rows of CDs in their long boxes with professionally-created signs guiding the customers to find *exactly* what they're looking for.

How indoor mall.

The old listening station is gone, along with its can of Lysol, replaced with a large, lice-free booth with only digital options.

The old cash register with yellowing *Bloom County* cartoons taped to the sides has been removed in favor of an updated version, complete with a wand scanner and a cash-drawer equipped for more impressive sales than just two to three a day.

The ALTERNATIVE section has been eliminated entirely and replaced with a WORLD MUSIC sign.

The GIVE A PENNY, TAKE A PENNY box has been thrown away. Best of lucky to anyone wanting to buy a CD Single and not having the final three cents!

Half the store is devoted entirely to Nirvana's *Nevermind*, one wall entirely covered with a fresh mural of a baby underwater, swimming not towards a dollar on a fishing hook … but to a *compact disc*.

Number One Records has officially transformed into *Number One Digital Music Express*.

So this is commercialism, Willow thinks. *It's so … shiny.*

And bright.

And dully effective.

Truth be told, there *are* certain elements to the re-design that Willow doesn't mind, such as the new bathroom with real soap.

But some elements, like the updated security system to prevent theft, she could do without. What was so wrong with the old security system, the one involving Skip chasing down customers to their deaths with a shotgun if anyone legally purchased a compact disc by Mike + The Mechanics?

That system worked pretty *damn well.*

The front door opens.

The opening chords to the new song again resounds.

Mr. Straight laughs as he enters the store and sings happily along to Eric Clapton's "Tears in Heaven."

So *that's* the song, Willow thinks.

"Love this song!" says Mr. Straight. "So *pretty*!"

Perhaps Mr. Straight is missing the song's basic point.

Next to him is his office assistant, a young male carrying a Korean BBQ grill with attached propane tank.

Mr. Straight motions to Willow to follow him into the back office. Not so much as a *hello* or even a *how are you* or a single *I masturbated to your image on the way over here*. No. Just a *follow me to the back office*. Willow has no choice but to follow.

Willow recognizes the assistant as Trust Exercises Ben from Mr. Straight's office.

"This is the most popular food in Seattle!" brags Mr. Straight. "Korean BBQ. You ever hear of this stuff? It's so new, Korea doesn't even have it! You grill it *yourself*! *Indoors*!"

"I'm not hungry," says Willow.

"Why?" asks Mr. Straight.

"Exhausted from all the work," admits Willow.

Is this what her parents do day after day? Hour after hour?

Work?

If the answer is yes, she has a newfound respect for anybody who has to work more than four hours a week.

Or at all.

"This is where you cook your food," says Mr. Straight. "You put the raw meat and you place it on the griddle. *Here*. Like *this*."

Trust Exercises Ben seizes a piece of raw chicken off a plate with a pair of metallic tongs and aggressively positions the translucent flesh on to the griddle.

Steam wafts toward the low ceiling above.

Typically—say yesterday or even the day before—Willow would have been astonished by the uniqueness of all it all. *Grilling indoors!*

"I expect the earnings to be *outrageous* today," says Mr. Straight. "Much *higher* than forecast!"

"That's nice," says Willow.

"Did you have fun last night?" asks Mr. Straight, thrusting towards Willow a plate of raw beef and a pair of tongs. "Helping to set up the new store?"

She holds a piece of raw beef to the overhead lights, so thin she can practically see through to the underwater baby mural beyond. She could have made Steak-umms at home for a lot cheaper.

But she will say this about Mr. Straight, unlike

Toody: *He never actually has a problem with actually paying.*

"No," says Willow. "Not fun."

Willow places the raw beef back down onto the plate. She's far from hungry.

Regardless, she could use to lose a few more pounds off her 85 pound frame.   *heroin chic*

"This is just business," Mr. Straight says.

"You told me that already."

Ben awkwardly shifts the raw chicken and meat around on the steaming grill for his boss.

"But you don't seem to grasp what I'm saying. I'm doing you a *favor*. I could have put any of my workers into this vital role. I didn't. I'm putting *you* here. Because you have *capability*."

"My *capability* is capturing my generation on digital tape," says Willow. "By the way, I threw out your condom tie."

Mr. Straight sighs. "Was hoping you wouldn't."

"Did."

Ben places a fresh piece of raw beef on the grill. The sizzle is strong.

"You're going to do a great job today. You have a real knack. We're going to break five figures."

"Is that good?"

"For an opening day, that would be *terrific*."

"I really liked you, Kevin," says Willow. "I really did."

"No longer?"

She sways a bit. The raw chicken and beef fumes are making her woozy. She wishes she had a gas mask.

205

Like those American soldiers overseas or wherever. "You know, you were different. Granted, your mixed tape was garbage—"

"It was?" He looks hurt.

He places a bit of cooked beef with chopsticks into his mouth.

"I'm sorry. It wasn't ... it just wasn't what I'm *used* to."

"What are you used to?"

"Music that's ... good?"

"I see."

"Kevin, why am I disregarding my own dreams? So *you* can make more money?"

"*We* make money," he says. "*We*. The more I make, the more *you* make."

"I don't *want* to make money."

"How are you going to live? Skin-jamming off your parents' Exxon card? Willow, whether we carry on or not into the future as lovers—"

Lovers?! she thinks. *Her grandparents were lovers. Her parents were lovers. Her generation does not have lovers ...*

"... I'd still like to work with you in a *Business* sense. Just think what it could do for your documentary! More money for it! A more professional feel. Better editing. Even a soundtrack with current, hot bands!"

Willow says nothing. The man just doesn't get it. She stopped using her father's Exxon card days ago.

Besides, the whole purpose of her stupid documentary is that it's supposed to look cheap! To make an

*expensive documentary about her generation would
be like carving a marble statue of a toothpick!*

Incredibly cool but …

"And Skip?" she asks.

"What about him?" Mr. Straight answers.

"Where does he fit into all this?"

"*Snugly.* Let's be honest: the guy could lose some
weight. Too much Chinese takeout."

"No. Seriously. Where do you think he fits?"

"I have enough worries."

"He's despondent. He left early. He's probably
home right now eating take-out Chinese listening to
Hoodoo Gurus. He could be doing that *here*."

"Good help, you know? *So hard to find.*"

"That's not funny, Kevin."

Attached to Mr. Straight's chin is a gristled, stri-
ated strand of beef, like a suicidal man on the verge
of leaping from a downtown skyscraper's window.

Willow can't take her gaze away from the gelati-
nous nightmare. The gristled strand drops even lower.

Don't jump!

"Willow, if I may be so bold ... what is your relationship with Toody? I really don't mean to pry but—"

"Is there a reason why you're asking?"

The gristle on Mr. Straight's gives up all hope …
and drops forlornly on to the grill. It splatters and
steams.

Willow prays the grill just cauterized whatever
the hell it used to be.

"I wanted to know if you'd come home with me
tonight. To have sexual relations."

Sexual relations?

With his tong, Ben flips the gristle, now burning, over on the grill and places the strand directly into Mr. Straight's mouth.

"Is this a joke?" Willow asks, waving away the smoke and odorous steam.

"No. *Not* a joke."

"You just act like an asshole and I have to follow?"

"Yes," says Mr. Straight. "This is how the real world *works*, Willow."

"Not *my* world," says Willow. "My world doesn't work like this at all."

"Your world isn't the *real* world," Mr. Straight says. "Mine is. You'll come to learn that."

"You know, Kevin, I've always meant to ask. What exactly did you do in the Environment before you got into the world of Business? You don't appear particularly the nurturing type."

He smiles. "Dolphins."

"Saving them?"

"I worked for the tuna industry."

"*Killing* dolphins?"

"I wouldn't put it that way. But if dolphins happened to be … sacrificed for our children's *nutritious* tuna sandwiches, well, then … I can live with that."

Willow nods. She should have known.

"You always intended to fire Skip, didn't you? You just wanted him for the transition. For him to sign over his store."

Mr. Straight shrugs. "I intended what I intended.

What can I say? Think over my offer. It'll stand in perpetuity. Headed home now to look over some more numbers. Get *cracking* today! You can *do* it!"

"Thanks," Willow mumbles.

"Cheer up. You're earning a living. You're now an adult. And facing adult problems. Speaking of which, fire Skip at your earliest convenience. Over and out."

He laughs.

"That was a joke, by the way."

"It was?" asks Willow.

"Um, no. Fire him."

Mr. Straight takes his barbecued Korean food and leaves the office.

It's only Willow now.

And Ben.

"He wants you to sleep with him," says Ben, after a long moment of silence.

"He does, yeah."

"But you've already slept with him."

"Is that a question?" asks Willow.

"No. I'm just saying, *You slept with that asshole already*."

"Okay," says Willow. "Yes. I made a mistake."

"You really did. He's awful."

"Then why are *you* working for him?"

Ben shrugs.

"Just the way the world works?" Willow asks, sadly, fanning the smoke and gagging a bit. She really *should* eat. It's going to be a long, exhausting, soul-sapping day.

"Yes, just the way the world works," Ben says,

grinning. "C'mere, let's eat."

Sunday, 8:07 P.M.

"Animated animals you'd most want to fuck," says Cody. "Paul Abdul's MC Skat Cat? Or Roger Rabbit?"

"Let's split the difference and say we'd like to fuck MC Skat but hang with Roger Rabbit." It's Topper. "Especially since Roger Rabbit was a dude."

"No problem there," says Wes, from the roof.

"Yeah," says Topper. "For *you*."

"Would never fuck a rabbit," says Cody. "I don't think so anyway."

The past few hours have been terribly trying. The Lost Boys' hearts just aren't in it.

Into anything.

Even barely existing has become strenuous!

Their beloved empty parking lot—their own Doin' Nothin' turf—has been filled from one end to the other with hordes of well-fed suburbanites, anxious to consume products, it really doesn't matter *what* products—at the world's most modernistic music store.

Word has spread quickly.

With barely enough room to skateboard within his own parking lot, Topper has given up entirely and sits forlornly on the curb.

Cody is now wearing a T-shirt with the Lucky the Charms Leprechaun. The creature is holding a NO MORE WAR IN NORTHERN IRELAND! sign. He resembles the world's #1 rock and roll star, Bono.

Tonight, it's Jack Jack's turn to be deliciously lazy. He's rented a hospital bed from a friend in the black market trade and now lies on it, blinking out responses like a locked-in stroke victim.

Royce, still woozy from all of the illegal medical experiments, is spray-painting the record store brick wall. It reads:

GO BACK VULTURES! WANNA FIGHT?!!

The G and T in FIGHT are backwards and upside down.

Bad.

Ass.

"No more wax," Bake says sadly. "Only CDs. It's all ones and zeros now." He ducks as Royce's spray-paint comes perilously close.

"CDs have been out for nearly ten years, guys," says Topper. "It's nothing new. Skip should have switched it up years ago."

He's ignored. It's more fun to be outraged.

"Supposedly, this is the most modern music store in existence," says Wes from the roof. His graduation robe is looking particularly tatty this afternoon. "This is 1999 level shit, yo!"

"Why do you sound so excited?" asks Topper, placing a Calvin Pissing on the American Flag sticker on the back of his skateboard. "Place sucks. Not what it used to be. As Bake says, No more wax. Meaning *records* are *kaput*! Never to return! *Gone*! *Finito*!"

"Do you own any records?" asks Bake.

"No. But … no more records," Topper says sadly.

"Where *is* Willow?" blinks out Jack Jack in Morse

212

code from the hospital bed. "Usually she's out here, *what?,* at least five times a stupid hour?"

He sits back.

He's dog-tired from all the blinking.

"Isn't she going to keep filming us?" asks Bake from the wall. "You know, to capture our generation for *posterior*-ority?"

"She's changed," says Wes. "*Different.* You know, from yesterday."

"Did you see Skip earlier? When he bolted from the store?" asks Topper. "Commercialism's *killing* that dude!"

"So Willow is still in there, running the place by *herself?*" asks Bake.

"Pretty much," says Topper. "Can't even *imagine* what's going on in there."

"Should we go in there and help her?" asks Bake. "But … this is hard for me to say …"

He gags.

"Work?" asks Topper. "You mean, like go in there and help her … by *working* with her?"

"Yeah. Go in there and help her with the … *work.*"

Topper's hands begin to violently shake. He tries to play it cool but he can't pull it off. He, too, gags.

"I'm thinking she'll close the store soon anyway," says Bake, hopefully.

"Yeah. I don't think we should go in there," agrees Cody. "And, you know, help her with …*work.*" He shivers.

"Yeah," agrees Jack Jack, through blinks. "No work."

213

"Maybe we should rush in quickly like they did in *Star Wars* and take advantage of the *one* weakness inside the Death Star to blow it all up," says Bake.

"The weakness being what exactly?" asks Cody.

"Her not wanting to work?" suggests Wes.

"*Us* not wanting to work?" suggests Bake.

They all contemplate the idea. Forget it. It's a terrific idea but *way* too much effort.

"I heard a rumor that Toody is dating the syphilitic penis," says Cody.

"That's not what I heard," says Wes, from the roof. "I heard something completely different."

"What did you hear exactly?" asks Cody.

"That he's dating the oozing vagina."

"I don't remember that costume," says Spooner.

"Costume?" asks Wes.

"And is Willow still seeing Mr. Straight?" asks Spooner.

"Not from what I've heard," says Wes, from the roof. "Heard Willow is absolutely *furious*. That she's back to being single."

"Now where do you hear all this?" asks Royce. "You never leave the damn roof!"

"Won't either—until my parents come and apologize for kicking me out of the house for being gay!"

"Right," says Spooner. "But where are you hearing all this gossip?"

Wes shrugs.

The truth is that he's been sleeping with the male producer of this film.

(Sadly this isn't something one can reveal for, say,

214

another fifteen years or so.)

The pay phone rings.

Wake walks over and picks up the receiver—but remains mute.

"Hello?" says a voice on the other end.

Wake taps the phone once for "yes." It's his phone code.

"Hello? *Anyone there*?" asks the voice on the other end. "*Hello*?!"

Wake drops the phone, which doesn't travel far. It swings to and fro, until Royce wombles over: "Define irony or I'll crack ya to the head, crackhead!"

"Hello?" says the voice on the other end. "*Hello*?"

Royce makes the game-show buzzer sound for "wrong answer."

"Hello?" the voice asks again. "Jesus! *Anyone*?!"

Royce whistles the tune for Final Jeopardy.

"You must define irony or I am hanging up," Royce says eventually.

"Is Willow there, please?" asks the voice. "Please. We *must* talk with her."

Male. Mainstream. No time for fun. Stinks of Boomer gone bad.

"She's *working*," says Royce and hangs up. And then to the rest: "That was Willow's dad."

"Why is he calling?" asks Wes.

"Didn't ask," says Royce. "Didn't feel like it. God, I could use a fight."

"Should I go tell her?" asks Topper. "Inside, where she's … *working*?"

"You want to brave that steaming shit hole?" asks

215

Wes. "I wouldn't even go in there with a hot-zone suit!"

"Not thrilled about heading into my *own* store," says Topper. "Let alone *hers*."

"How bad?" asks Royce.

"Had to get rid of all my videos with three characters on the cover, in black trench coats, standing in a triangle, pointing a handgun at each other."

"Jesus," says Cody. "*Fucking monsters*. My condolences."

"And it'll now be open three hours a day, not two."

"Renting what?"

"Videos featuring Julia Roberts running from the Supreme Court with a sheaf of papers."

Cody can only nod once. *No words.*

He's sickened.

A stretch limousine enters the parking lot.

"Looks like our Tony Stark has returned!" says Royce. "I knew he would!"

"Isn't he speaking tonight?" asks Cody, sitting on the garbage can. "At the hacky-sack convention over at the coliseum?"

"Thought so," said Royce. "But, you know, who can blame him? Couldn't stay away. We bring him too much … *pleasure*."

"Billionaire Iron Man," says Wes. "Now I'd suck *that* iron dick."

"You've said that already," says Spooner.

"True, but I'd suck it *again*," says Wes. "I would get down on my knees like a little naughty baby seal and …" He gets down on his knees—not the safest of positions on a sloped roof—and proceeds to blow an imaginary iron dick. *"Uhmpa, uhmpa, uhmpa ... "*

"Bigger dick: Ultra-Man or Mothra?" blinks out Jack Jack.

"Ultra-Man by a goddamn mile," answers Cody. "Dig ol' bick throwing sparks!"

The long stretch white limousine slows to a crawl and double parks next to the Lost Boys. The motor stays on.

"Doesn't look the same," says Royce. "This limo looks bigger."

"Jesus. Somebody even *more* important," says Topper excitedly.

The engine revs, smoke cinematically billowing.

And then, from out of a rear door, a beautiful woman exits holding a microphone. A middle-aged male assistant and cameraman tags just behind, capturing all.

"Is this Seattle?" the red-headed woman asks the Boys.

"You're standing smack dab *within* it," says Wes from the roof. "*Knee* deep."

"Ha!" the woman laughs. "That is precisely what I assumed someone from Seattle might say! Negative, sarcastic talk. I *adore* it! Angry! Pointed! *Unnecessary*!"

"And who might we be?" asks Wes. "This visitor to our foreign land?"

"My name is Tabitha."

"Tabitha," says Wes. "*Tabitha*?"

"The ... *Tabitha* on TV?" asks Royce. "We used

to watch you in Iraq. Holy shit, *holy shit*! We beat off to you!"

"I must look different in real life," she says, smiling. "Yes, the one you saw on TV in Iraq. And … the one you … beat off to."

"Hell are you doing here?" blinks out Jack Jack.

"What?" asks Tabitha. "What did he just do with his eyes?"

Tabitha S, she was famous DJ from MTV 1990s

"Why here?" Jack Jack blinks out slower.

"What did he just say?" asks Tabitha. "Is he trying to communicate with his eyes?"

"He's asking," says Royce, "what you are doing here. In this parking lot? In Seattle?"

"We're here for a major televised event. We were driving past … and *couldn't* resist. This place … this place looks to be dead center within the Grunge Zone!"

"Grunge Zone?" says Topper. "What's a *Grunge Zone*?"

"Would that be like the *Dead* Zone?" asks Cody. "Second favorite Stephen King book. Just behind *The Shining*. Movie not superior to the book, by the way. I can tell you why if you got a few days."

Tabitha ignores him.

Reality's a bummer.

Cody heads straight for the pay phone. He desperately needs a daydream to boost his spirits.

Like stat!

Tabitha turns to her male assistant. "This'll do just fine."

"Just fine for what?" asks Wes, from the roof.

"For the Great MTV Grunge Off," she replies, eyeing the parking lot. "The manager of the methadone clinic said no. So ... this is where we've ended up. *Kizmet*." She turns to her assistant. "We have sixteen hours. You think we can make it?"

Her assistant nods glumly.

Topper zooms past on his black skateboard, jumps off the curb, performing a 180, minus (give or take) about 80 degrees, and nails the landing.

Wicked!

"You boys ready to do an honest day's work?" Tabitha asks.

"Huh?" asks Topper.

He literally does not understand the question.

"Would you be interested in turning this parking lot into a live concert venue by, say, 4:00 P.M. tomorrow?"

"*Whaaaaaaaa?*" blinks out Jack Jack.

"I am asking if you would be willing to *work* for money?" asks Tabitha. "You know? *Doing things*? And then you would be *paid* for doing those things?"

What is wrong with this crew? she thinks. *Not at all like the easily-stimulated crowd sitting on the high school bleachers in the latest Nirvana video!*

At least those dimwits had energy!

"Money?" asks Spooner. "To *buy* things?"

"Like cheddar popcorn in sealed bags?" asks Royce.

"Sure," says Tabitha, patiently. "Like cheddar popcorn in sealed bags."

"Then we're in!" blinks out Jack Jack, excitedly.

He lies back on his rented hospital bed. Maybe his father was wrong, after all! Maybe he *isn't* allergic to "good old-fashioned work"! Maybe his only allergy is to becoming a "traditional success."

"Okay then," says Tabitha. "Then … you guys... get to *work*!"

Cody is over at the pay phone, speaking animatedly with an operator from 1-900-DAY-DREA for an emergency consultation. Her daydream recommendation this time is for Cody to become the first astronaut to ever oversleep and miss blastoff. *The women of the world will absolutely love his insouciance!*

He'll now be paid extremely well to sign autographs at comic-book conventions!

Not bad!

This ought to take his mind off the Tabitha snub quite nicely!

"Tell me more," Cody says, plunking additional quarters into the slot. "A *lot* more…"

Tabitha walks back over to the stretch limousine. She dials on her IBM Simon, the second of only three in the world. The third is owned by the world's richest man, Donald Trump.

The battery lasts for one full hour!

Plenty of time for Tabitha to call MTV headquarters back in New York and give them the 4-1-1.

That means "information."

Meanwhile …

Sunday, 8:16 P.M.

Willow exits the store with Ben after a very long day.

Mr. Straight had been right: they pulled in five figures.

Willow presses PLAY on her Fuji DS-100 digicam with 3-power zoom. She intends to apologize to the Lost Boys for her absence and capture their reaction. She's been away far too long.

It feels good to be *creative* again!

The more she thinks about it, the more she considers that commercialism really isn't for her, although there *were* a few aspects that she semi-enjoyed, such as dealing with actual money and being able to flush after going number twoskies—

Hang on. She notices someone new in the parking lot, talking to the Lost Boys...

Another woman?

With red hair?

Is that who she thinks it is?

Red hair aflame with fame?

Standing casually with a microphone by a limousine?

"Oh my god," Willow mutters.

Tabitha?

From the TV?

No last name needed? (Or allowed because of legal reasons?)

Is she here because I just worked eight hours?

Whatever the reason, Willow nearly faints.

Like staring straight into the sun.

Or licking a rainbow.

Or riding the Mall of America's indoor roller-coaster after eating a bucket of fried clams.

It is *her*. She can't believe it! Willow knows Tabitha even *better* than she knows her *own* self!

"Hi. I'm Tabitha," says the red-haired woman, approaching and holding a microphone.

Like Willow didn't know!

The mic is thrust into Willow's face. "What's your name?"

"My name is Willow," says Willow, thrusting *her* camera in Tabitha's face. "Am I ... am I being interviewed?"

"No," says Tabitha. "Am I?'

"No," says Willow, smiling.

The two women face off.

"Then what are you doing?"

"Then what are *you* doing?"

"This is what I do. I'm Tabitha."

"And this is what *I* do. I'm Willow. I'm capturing the greatness of my generation for … MTV."

"You're capturing *our* generation?" asks Tabitha.

Our generation. Not *your* generation. But *our*.

Willow loves the way that just sounded. *She is part of the same generation as Tabitha! Together, they are changing the world!*

Together!

"Tell me more about capturing *our* generation."

"For the past two weeks I've been … shooting endless digital footage of my friends."

"Who are your friends?"

Willow launches into it. She's long ago had it memorized:

"This is Willow Montgomery and I am twenty-three years old. I wasn't born in Seattle but I moved here *before* all the poseurs arrived. I'd like to introduce you to a few of my finest friends in the entire world. I would like to think we're all incredibly special. I think you will soon feel the same. This is a *revolution*! Start it off, Spooner!"

"Darth Vader was Paul," says Spooner, slapping a shot into a makeshift net fashioned from white tubing stolen from behind a medical supply store. The shot misses. The puck is a yet another AOL free-trial CD, one of millions that litter the lot and the entire universe.

"*These* guys?" asks Tabitha.

From his rented hospital bed, Jack Jack blinks: "Yes, *these* guys! Is there anyone available to *fluff* my pillow, please?"

Over at the pay phone, Cody hangs up. He takes a bite out of his slice of pizza, a huge one. He places the slice back down on to a dirty surface within the phone booth. It'll be safe until he returns. He blades over to the curb, mouth full, and sits with a loud sigh. His energy for the day is sapped. But he still has some daydreaming to do: *Cody is attending a comic-book convention dressed as an astronaut. He's wearing a round, glass helmet so popular in the 1950s and early 1960s before man ever went into space. Beautiful women turn to look as he struts onto the scene.* "Hello, ladies," *he says through his helmet mic.* "Anyone want to 'do it'?"

"Yes," answers Willow. "*These* guys!"

"May I see what you have so far produced?" says Tabitha. "To capture our generation?"

Willow presses "EJECT." Out pops a large 10-byte flash-memory card.

Across it, written in marker, is: CAPTURING MY GENERATION #184!

"May I keep it?" asks Tabitha, already pocketing the memory card.

"Yes … of course," says Willow, too stunned to move. Out of reflex, she smacks a brand new 10-byte flash-memory card right back into the camera and starts recording.

Locked and reality loaded!

Why would Tabitha herself show up in a dinky town like Seattle and thrust a long mic into Gen X'ers faces and not have sent a second-string, backup VJ for the job? It can only mean one thing: Willow made the correct decision to forgo a full ride to Yale Law to capture this incredible magic!

"Well, wonderful to meet you, Willow," says Tabitha. "Thank you for allowing this to happen. I will see you tomorrow. Let's change the world. *Together*."

Together.

Willow gets the chills. The mic enters the limousine first, followed by Tabitha.

"Wait!" says Willow. "Exactly what am I *allow-*

224

ing to happen?"

Tabitha leans her head out. "The Great Grunge Off. Here. In the parking lot. Tomorrow at 4:00 P.M. Do we have your permission?"

"Do you really need my permission?"

"Are you the manager of this record store?"

"I am … yes."

"Then, yes, we *need* your permission. Do we have it?"

"My boyfriend—" Willow starts, and then corrects herself. It's going to take awhile to get used to this. "That is, my *ex* boyfriend is performing at the Grunge Off. His name is Toody."

"*Toody.*"

"Yeah. Toody."

"I'll keep an eye out for him. But do we have your permission?"

Yes," says Willow. "As manager of this record store—"

She clears her throat.

"Um, as manager of this *compact disc* store, you have my permission."

"Very good," says Tabitha. "You know, I'm recognizing a lot of my younger traits in you. Initiative. Perseverance. A sense of entitlement that has no bearing on reality. I *love* it."

With that, she points to the driver, a middle-aged man wearing a chauffeur's cap that reads "Mister Loder." He appears none too happy with his assistant role.

After the stretch pulls out of the parking lot with a

loud squeal, Topper turns to the Lost Boys. "C'mon."

"Yeah," states Jack Jack. "I never thought I'd ever say this but … we have work to do."

He then retches.

Is Willow dreaming?

Or being programmed by a Radio Shack employee to think that she's dreaming?

Either way, the Lost Boys and Willow get to work.

This is Seattle.

This is the early 1990s.

It is *electrifying*.

"Anyone?" blinks out Jack Jack. "Pillow? *Fluff*? *Please*?!"

They all laugh.

Not tonight, sir.

No.

Tonight is for … working.

Jack Jack blinks: "Fuck off."

Everyone laughs. It is extremely funny.

But then they stop laughing.

There is *work* to be done!

They get to work.

It really is time to get to work.

Monday, 1:04 A.M.

"That was awful," says Bake, from the wall.

"*Horrific*," says Mac. "Wasn't anywhere near as great as almost shaking hands with the Dalai Lama. Not even close to that."

"Where's Matt Dillon?" asks Becca. "I was told he'd be wearing an unrealistic grunge wig while shooting a very bad movie."

"Hey, guys," says Willow, still in the parking lot, sweeping. "I didn't say this would be *fun*. I said this would be … *work*."

"I'm exhausted from all the observing," says Wes, from the roof.

"Then maybe you should get down here and *help*," says Topper.

"Are you criticizing my anti-homophobia protest?" asks Wes, a bit petulantly.

"I'm saying that you should get down and help," says Topper. "We could *use* it."

"And why are we doing this again?" asks Royce to Willow. "It's only going to benefit Mr. Straight's horrible store. And more assholes coming to this city."

Next to the trash can, Topper is busy pushing a small mound of trash with a stick, back and forth, back and forth. He reminds Willow of a monkey poking impotently at an ant hill with its own tail.

"Guys, *guys*," says Willow.

She's never seen the Lost Boys argue in the entire

227

two weeks she's know them. "This is *incredibly* important."

"Why?" asks Topper.

"To show the world what Seattle is made of. To show what *we're* made of. To prove that we are experiencing a *revolution*. Yes, the store will do better business. But we'll *all* be better off."

"And maybe to show MTV what *you're* made of?" blinks out Jack Jack from the rented hospital bed. "Could that also be why you want to do this? For selfish reasons?"

"Maybe," says Willow. "Yes. Would that be so bad? That I don't have to live off my father's Exxon credit card anymore?"

"Maybe," blinks out Jack Jack. "*Perhaps*. But you are working for a dipshit."

"That's part of being an adult," says Willow, not convincingly.

"I *hate* this," says Vicky. "I *hate* working."

For sure, the past hour has been more strenuous than stapling concert flyers to telephone polls. It also didn't help that Vicky walked the two miles from her apartment in a pair of corrective, club-foot shoes after receiving the following beeper code:

"MTV in town. Please help set up for the Grunge Off so that MTV may purchase my documentary and so that I may become the voice of my generation."

It was a complicated message and Vicky at first misread it to mean "Suck Tabitha's ass as the lightning strikes," which excited her, but, regardless, she is here and helping.

Hardly anything has been accomplished but they barely tried.

And now, a few hours later, they've all had enough. The Lost Boys retreat back to their particular stations and Vicky and Willow make their way home through the gloomy streets, each alone with her own thoughts and yet both warmed by the other's presence.

There's nothing like a good friend of barely two weeks to keep your mood buoyed o'er the choppy waters of post-grad malaise!

"*Incredible* night," says Vicky. "You did a fantastic job! I just know Tabitha is going to be over the moon!"

"I think she'll be happy with the way things turned out," says Willow, a bit modestly, sticking out a thumb. "We worked really kinda-hard." A car passes.

"*Huge* responsibility," says Vicky. "The biggest of our lives! Except for the stage and chairs and everything else we never dealt with."Another car passes

She looks over to Willow, who appears glum.

"Are you still upset by what the Lost Boys were throwing your way earlier?"

"These are my friends. I turned my back on them, Vips. They do have a point. I wasn't there for them today. That's not like me. Maybe I *have* gone commercial. It can happen to anyone. And what am I going to do about Skip? Just leave him hanging in what used to be his store?"

"Turned your back on them how?" Vicky asks. "What do they know about anything? One's been perched on a damn roof for two weeks! And Skip ran the store into the ground. Maybe this is a *good* thing."

"Skip ran it the way he wanted it run. That's *free-dom*. As for Wes, he's protesting homophobia."

"Come on."

"He has conviction, you have to admit that."

"Definitely conviction," says Vicky. "Just not sure it's placed correctly."

"He's gay," Willow patiently explains. "He's different than the rest of us. He's … *moody*. But we should love him anyway."

Vicky nods. Willow is exceedingly beautiful and can also be so very wise!

"I took away the only home the Lost Boys ever wanted," continues Willow. "Where will they now do absolutely nothing in the future?"

"I'm sure they'll find a new parking lot."

"But it won't be *our* parking lot."

"It'd have been somebody else if not you," says Vicky. "This city is changing. We're grandfathered in, you know that. We arrived minutes before the video aired. But you're an *adult* now. So this is what an adult must deal with."

"What exactly do I *deal* with?" asks Willow dramatically. "Besides working a retail McJob and having no boyfriend?"

"If you wanted, you could have either Toody or Mr. Straight in a Seattle second," says Vicky.

"Not sure I'd want either. Mr. Straight is a jerk. And Toody is barely capable of remaining cognizant." She pauses dramatically. "I suppose that's the matter with our generation. We don't know *what* we want. And when we do, we *still* don't want it." theme

230

"But you managed to capture it so well on 10-byte flash-memory card."

Willow nods. *Truth*.

"You're one to talk," Willow says. "You're always saying you're so lonely. Skip worships the club-footed shoes you barely walk on."

"Guy's got no game," says Vicky. "I need someone more like DJ Truth." grunge slang

"Fantasy," says Willow. "Bring it down to earth. Like an *adult*."

"DJ Truth was talking to *me*, I know it."

"He's talking to *everyone*. That's his *job*."

Vicky and Willow continue to counter-swing on the flippity-flop through the clackity-clack down-townity area.

Willow thinks: *My graduation present should have been a goddamn car! Not a stupid Fuji DS-100 digicam with 3-power zoom!*

But then she catches herself. *What is she talking about? She's doing this for all of humanity! It's time that Willow appreciates Willow!* true

A GMC Pickup drives past, Sammy Hagar blasting. The driver is wearing a pair of white overalls. It's one of the unionized Oompa Loompas. Willow quickly puts her thumb down. The pickup passes.

The thumb goes back up.

Another car approaches, windows open, radio blasting. This car, too, passes without stopping.

"Did you hear that?" asks Vicky.

"Hear what? Ace of Bass?"

"No. A *voice*. From the *radio*."

"I didn't hear a thing, Vicky. I just want to get home and Judy Blume myself into infinity—" masturbate?!!

"Wait a second," says Vicky. "That … *that* was DJ Truth!"

Vicky hobbles after the car but it's already taken a right onto Union Street, towards I-5. "Did you hear that! *DJ Truth!*"

"I'm not so sure it was, Vaz," says Willow, slowly. "It could have been *anyone* on the radio!"

"Oh, it definitely was," says Vicky. "I can recognize that voice, blindfolded, with an S&M red rubber ball up my ol' yazoo."

"*What*?" asks Willow.

"1989 frat party," continues Vicky.

"Ah," says Willow.

Most of Vicky's stories end, or begin, with the phrase "1989 frat party."

Another car passes, windows open, radio blaring. Now even Willow can hear it. "That *is* DJ Truth!" she screams. "*Everyone's* listening to him! You were right, Vicky! You aren't delusional!"

"*Stop*!" Vicky calls after the car but it's already speeding ahead. "Hey! *Stop*! We just want to *listen*!"

"Damnit!" yells Willow. She breaks into a run but quickly stops.

Enough with the mainstream running shit.

The mist thickens and cliches.

It's difficult, if not impossible, to see a few feet into the fog but Willow can hear something just around the corner. "I can hear something, Willow," she says, pushing forward.

Vicky struggles to catch up. "Wait for me, Wilps!"

When Vicky finally turns the corner, she notices hundreds of cars parked next to each other in a lot.

All windows are up.

All doors are open.

Seemingly thousands of teenagers and twenty-somethings stand outside their cars, smiling.

All stations are tuned to 88.3.

Typical Gen-Xer's!

All listening to the same radio station at the same time—and in *public*!

"This is *incredible*!" says Vicky.

"*Magical*!" says Willow.

DJ Truth is speaking to all of Seattle! As usual, he is using a harmonizer to disguise his voice: *"And I don't typically talk about my friends, such as Skip. But this particular childhood friend, this friend I've been going on about for the past few hours, is special."*

"What's going on?" whispers Willow, to one of the listeners.

"Shhhhhhh!" someone replies.

"My god, he really *does* know Skip," says Vicky. "I can't believe it!"

"Shhhhh!" someone else replies.

"See, for me, Skip represents what this city was like before the hordes arrived. Before a certain British journalist who shall go unnamed coined a word which shall also go unnamed. This is a live show tonight. You just heard the first side of Black Flag's My War. *But this isn't my war. This is* our *war. Those who can truly call themselves Seattle-ites ..."*

hes talking about the **233** word grunge british
writer came up w/ the name

"That's us," whispers Vicky to Willow, who nods. "We were grandfathered in!"

"Under the *Smells Like Teen Spirit Act*!" finishes Willow.

" ... *will wake up, shake off the sleep, and take a look around. What do you see? I see a city that desperately needs to be summoned like a phoenix and take its messy self back from outsiders!*"

"Is he calling for war?" asks Willow. ☺

"I'm not calling for war ..." says DJ Truth, voice garbled.

"Thank god," says Vicky.

" ... *what I am calling for is all of the love and decency and goodness that is within you, your positive energy, your good feelings, I want you to take all that and harness it to win a much-needed fight over corporate greed ... this is our Watergate, at last ...*"

Vicky nearly swoons. finally has something to fight for

" ... *I'm talking about getting into your vehicles! Or your recumbent bikes! And make your way to where, until yesterday, the Number One Vinyl store sat! And I want you to make a difference! ...*"

"I hate that place," says a man, standing next to his Buick Electra.

"Me, too," says a man wearing tie-dyed karate pants. "Mean as shit. Once chased me out for buying a *Best Of UB-40*."

"Just crappy alternative garbage," says a man wearing an umbrella hat.

Now it's Willow's turn to shush.

There's no need here for the truth here! Especially

when talking over DJ Truth!

"... I want you to overlook any potential differences you might have had over the years with Skip when it comes to ... music. *Sure, Skip can at times be ... emotional over things he truly and deeply loves. Like all of us ..."*

A car at the entrance to the lot revs and peels out. It's soon followed by another.

" ... so show your love for me. *Show your love* for Skip. *Show your love for our* Seattle ..."

Willow instinctively sticks out her thumb. The driver of the car idling next to her, one of the hundreds of cars not yet moving and hemmed in by all the other cars not yet moving, leans his head out the driver's side window and asks a bit wearily, "Ride?"

"Where you headed?" asks Vicky.

"To the record store," he responds, exhausted. "Where everyone else is going. You knew that. Get in."

In truth, there's not much else to do at 1:00 A.M. in Seattle on a Monday morning.

"It's the *revolution*!" screams Willow to Vicky, opening the back door. "C'mon, Vulps!"

"Hit it!" Vicky yells, taking the backseat. "Start it off! *Kick off this revolution*!"

The car remains idling. It won't be another forty, forty-five minutes until it exits the parking lot to metaphorically "hit it."

It won't be another twenty, twenty-five minutes until they arrive anywhere close to Skip's store to kick off this amazing revolution.

But, by the time they finally do arrive, Vicky and Willow will find that hell has already broken loose!

Monday, 2:11 A.M.

Nothing much is happening.

The lot is jammed econo from end to end with Ford Explorer Eddie Bauers.

And tents—lots of tents. Most with protest flags and signs attached.

The hand-made signs are so much more refreshing and hip than the professionally-created ones inside of a compact disc store.

Authentic.

More *valid.*

Circling the Number One Digital Music Express are seemingly hundreds of twenty-somethings, chanting, linking their arms together, preventing any customers from entering.

"*What do we want*!" scream the circled protestors.

"*Our Seattle back*!" comes the reply from long-time Seattleites.

"When do we want it!"

"*Now*!"

"Incredible," exclaims Vicky. "A true revolution! Our parents had their wars. We have … *this.*"

"Then again, we did have the Drug Wars," says Vicky. "And that was exciting."

Willow knew it would happen one day. She's not sure what, exactly, but *something.*

Anything.

Literally. Please.

Something!

Willow now points to a huge crowd of suburban-ites protesting on the *other* side of the lot.

This group is protesting that the new, sparkly version of the store shall remain *open*.

"*What* do we want?!"

"Nirvana!" is the answer. "*When* do we want it?"

"Now!" is the answer. "*Entertain* us!"

A streaker takes off through the crowd.

A grunge streaker!

A cheer arises to the low heavens above. He is walking. The crowd adores it.

"Excuse me," the streaker says to Vicky. "I need to streak on by."

He passes very slowly.

Radios are everywhere, inside cars and out, all sizes, all on, but none bigger than a boom box and none smaller than a transistor.

DJ Truth's voice can be heard, louder now and even more confident: "*If you can't fight for what is yours, what exactly can you fight for? Rise up! Smash the hierarchy! But let's do it our way!*"

"DJ Truth!" says Vicky, clearly impressed. "The power of pirate radio!"

"*Rise up! Rise up! Rise up!*" chants DJ Truth, through the voice harmonizer. "*Shut it down, shut it down, shut it down!*"

"Leave the store *as is*!" screams the suburbanites and jocks from the suburbs. "*As is! As is! As is*!"

"*Bring back the way it was!*" scream the true Seat-tle-ites. "*Before the outsiders invaded!*"

"We may never see anything so powerful again!" pipes in Willow. "I can't *imagine* human beings ever being able to spread the word so effectively! This is *futuristic*!" she doesnt know whats coming

"But what are you going to do?" asks Vicky. "You're the *manager*! Should you keep the store as is? Or return it to what it once was?" dilemma?

"How can I return it to its former self?" asks Willow. "I'm just the manager. Mr. Straight is the owner!"

"Then go protect it," says Vicky. "That would be your job as a manager, right?"

"I suppose I must," says Willow. But then her face collapses. "Oh, Vuppers!" She begins to weep as might a child. "What would Cliff Huxtable do?"

It's a question that carries a tremendous amount of weight. In essence, how would Jesus or Buddha act if either happened to be the manager of a compact disc store in a failing strip mall?

But Willow also knows that she is not helping matters by standing stock still next to a man wearing a paisley kimono and clinking a pair of finger cymbals over and over and over. More than that, the slow-moving streaker is approaching again.

Willow can see now why most streakers prefer to move quickly.

The paisleyed man clangs his tiny cymbals yet again.

I despise the Manchester sound, Willow thinks.

"You want to know what Cliff Huxtable would do? Well, Cliff Huxtable would confidently walk up to

239

that group of protestors," says Vicky, "and he would say in a strong, steady voice: 'I run this store. Let me through. I represent goodness. And being an *adult*. Let me through *please*.' And then, if it were *me* there and not Cliff Huxtable, I would say, 'Move your fucking asses, assholes! I am the fucking *boss*!'"

Willow manages a slight smile. "I think you're right, Vap. You always tell the truth because you're not as good looking as me. I think you're absolutely—"

just being honest

Tabitha, from out of nowhere, sidles up next to Willow. She's holding a clipboard and her IBM Simon.

"This is amazing!"

"It is?"

"*Perfect* for the cameras. What is *happening*?"

"DJ Truth called for people to mobilize against the record—er, *CD* store."

"And who are *those* people," Tabitha asks, pointing to the suburbanites.

"People who want the store to stay as it is."

"And who are *those* people," Tabitha asks.

"People who want the store to change back to what it once was."

Tabitha calls over her assistant, Mr. Loder.

"We're starting the Great American Grunge Off competition now, not tomorrow."

"Why now?" asks Willow.

"The mood is *perfect*. It's so grungy! Let's *do* this Grunge Off!"

"It's 2:11 AM."

"All the grungier!" says Tabitha.

A suburban BMW roars into the parking lot, finding the last space not blocked by pro-Palestinian pup tents.

A gasp escapes from the crowd.

"Oh no!" says Willow.

"Oh boy!" says Vicky, afraid to look but feeling she must.

It's Mr. Straight and he is enraged! Not even his powerful aftershave fragrance can mask *this* level of irritation!

He's even forgotten to put on a tie.

Poor thing resembles a bird hatched a day early.

"Let me through," he screams. "Into my own damn store!"

"I don't think so," says a new voice from the back. "You ain't goin' nowhere!"

"Oh no," says Willow. "It's Toody!"

"Oh boy," says Vicky.

"Here we go!" says Royce. "Fight time!"

"Are *you* going to fight?" asks Willow to Royce.

"Hell no," says Royce. "Just love to watch."

Toody emerges unhurriedly from out of the shadows. He's wearing black biking shorts over white long-johns severed violently just beneath the knee; a Generra cotton fabric shirt that magically turns into different colors based on Toody's current mood (bright red, as of now); a jacket bought at a Salvation Army store originally worn by a soldier who was killed or something or other overseas, or domestically, it probably doesn't matter, it looks just fantastic.

His shirt is buttoned once—at the very top, Chicano gangster style.

Toody is also wearing a wool ski cap. Perfect to protect the top of his head in this bitter 67 degree weather.

"I don't think so," Toody says again. "You ain't going nowhere!"

To the best of Willow's knowledge, nobody who's ever spoken through a super-fuzz distortion box carried around with a shoulder strap has ever won an argument.

Maybe President Nixon? Willow can't remember.

But Toody is giving it his best shot now.

Toody and Mr. Straight face off. These two have been waiting a *long* time for this!

"Been waiting for this," says Mr. Straight. "A *long* time!"

"You got nothin'," says Toody, through the distortion box. "*Intimidating*! *Younger*!!!!!!!!! Possibly *crazyyyyyyyy*!!!!"

Toody gets down into his singer lean, but not quite all the way, one leg jutted out at a sharp angle.

Mr. Straight bends his arms in front of himself in a fighting stance just like the angry mascot for Notre Dame.

"Let's do this!" asks Toody. He lets out a grunge scream: *"Anger! Arduously enacted fury! Fighting over my Willow!"*

Mr. Straight is circling like a professor at a business school speaking to an incoming, misbehaving freshman: "Why is she *yours*? She's nothing but a product that you will never be close to obtaining."

A product? thinks Willow.

"Product?! Outraged for the cameras! Ahhhhhhh-hhhhhhhhh! Bwa-faaaaa!!!!!!!!!!!!!!! We were meant for each other. Emotional turbulence!!!!!!!!!!!!"

"He's fighting for *me*," says Willow.

"Not effectively, but yes," says Vicky. "They're *both* fighting for you."

"Camera on *them*!" says Tabitha to her assistant, Mr. Loder, still wearing a chauffeur's hat.

Mr. Loder swings the camera over to the fighting twosome. "And we're live!" he announces.

"Poetry slam!" Toody says into an imaginary mic, taking it out of its imaginary stand. "Me versus *that* guy!"

He points to Mr. Straight.

Toody launches straight into it.

"Business*man*," he raps. "Business*man* with *zero* plan. Too *straight* to create. Uppity! Yippity! *Yop!* Diggity diggity *hop*—"

"No more poetry slams!" interrupts Mr. Straight. "This time we *fight*. For *real*!"

A hush goes through the crowd. *For real? A physical fight? When was the last time this happened in Seattle?*

"Physical, yes," says Mr. Straight. "For *real*."

Toody looks stunned. The last time he did anything "real," he ended up in traction.

But he guesses it's already been decided. And he's just too lazy to demonstrate.

The fight begins!

Attacking first is Mr. Straight, with an errant swing.

Next up is Toody, who slaps Mr. Straight.

243

The crowd laughs.

Together, Toody and Mr. Straight fall to the ground, kicking and screaming.

The crowd laughs harder.

"I *adore* this!" says Tabitha. "You getting this?"

Mr. Loder nods.

Even *he's* laughing.

"How long can this go on?" asks Willow.

"Hopefully all night," says Tabitha. "God, this is *perfection*!"

Toody gets down into a sprinter's crouch and takes off straight into Mr. Straight's chest—world's most ineffective stage dive attack.

They entangle and scrap like two baby squirrels.

"Are you okay, Wills?" asks Vicky, lightly grabbing Willow's arm. "Maybe I should just get you home. We'll watch more infomercials about the rope-and-pulley system men are using if they can't achieve a proper erection. *Squeak, squeak*!"

Willow doesn't laugh.

"That sounds fun, Vicky. But … *I can't*. I have responsibilities now. You know. Like running a record store that's no longer a record store."

"You've changed, Willow."

"Don't start," says Willow. "Please. I'm too *exhausted* too even—"

"For the better," finishes Vicky. "You've changed for the *better*, Willup."

Willow tears up. "Do you really think so, Vucks?"

"I do," says Vicky. "You're … more of an adult now. It's clear that you despise Mr. Straight, as well you should, but you also have a responsibility to run the record store. So you're going to do what's *right*. That's not a child talking ... that's an *adult*."

Willow hugs Vicky. It's the most beautiful thing she's been told since a homeless man with no bottom lip outside a Borders in the Bitter Lake district told her she had the "world's most beautiful labium."

The crowd is only growing larger. Willow estimates in the low millions ... but she could be slightly off.

"Then again," says Vicky. "You don't want to run the record store because it's not what it used to be. It's cold now. *Sterile*. And you feel you owe Skip. And the Lost Boys. *Dilemma*." *dilemma!!*

"Dilemma," repeats Willow. "It is a *dilemma*."

Toody lets out a loud screech. Mr. Straight has just bit him.

Toody slaps Mr. Straight across the face.

Mr. Straight shrieks.

There's a loud *pop*!

At first Willow fears it might be Toody's ear plug finally being dislodged from his right nostril. Or Mr. Straight's red suspenders exploding under the first physical strain he's experienced since Beer Pong Olympics at the Kappa Sigma basement junior year.

It's neither.

Rather, it's the sound of the klieg lights turning on—but from *behind* the strip mall, high atop a hillside that Willow never even knew existed. *Is the hill new?* It's an incredibly convenient spot for these blinding lights, almost cinematically so, blazing from the very top of the hill.

All protestors, whether from the suburbs or downtown, whether grunge or paisley, blading or lamely walking, within an iron lung or Type A enough to breathe on one's own, just back from a medical experiment to pay for convenience store food or having to protest on the roof for two weeks in order to combat homophobia, whether rooting for Toody or whether rooting for Mr. Straight, shield their eyes.

"What is *happening*?!" says Willow. "And where did that hill *come* from?"

A human figure, backlit by the powerful lights, begins a slow ascent down to the parking lot. Its shadow only increases in size as it descends …

Thousands of flashbulbs go off on modern one-use plastic cameras.

"Oh no," says Willow. "Is it going to *hurt* us?"

The mysterious shadow only grows larger and larger.

Toody and Mr. Straight stop fighting to look up.

"It's DJ Truth!" a woman in cat-eye glasses shrieks. Willow recognizes her from last week's Lisa Loeb concert. She was dancing alone.

"It *is* him!" screams a middle-aged man in pleated-jeans. Willow recognizes him from last week's Matthew Sweet's concert. He, too, was dancing alone.

Maybe these two will end up later dancing together? After he urinates a heart into a snowbank?

"It *is* me," says DJ Truth through the radios.

There's a hiss of feedback the closer he approaches.

"We done?" Toody asks Mr. Straight.

246

"Yeah," says Mr. Straight, re-adjusting a tie that's not there.

"Cool," says Toody, sweeping his dewy, shoulder-length hair behind his ears and gently massaging his mic hand.

Why fight if no one is looking?

And when a streaker is slowly walking over to referee?

"We're going to see who DJ Truth finally is," says Vicky, trembling. "I can't *believe* this! DJ Truth! This is like the dream sequence in *Barton Fink*."

And that's a good thing? Willow thinks.

"Don't trust him!" someone screams. "Don't trust DJ Truth! He's the *devil*!"

"The devil?!" someone asks. "*Where*?!"

The shadowed creature descends lower. Its head elongates, its hands stretch to infinity, lower, lower—

"Swing the camera *that* way," says Tabitha to Mr. Loder. "*Real* tight shot now, c'mon, let's not miss this!"

And what happens next re-sets the course of humankind forever.

Monday, 4:25 A.M.

The klieg lights on top of the hill flick off with a *thwak* and the mysterious pirate DJ, no longer backlit, is exposed for all the world to see.

A scream erupts.

"My god," says Willow. "*Skip*?"

Skip takes a deep breath. "Yes. It's me. I am DJ Truth. I always have been." *always has been DJ truth*

Skip knew these lights would one day come in handy.

He's loved them in every concert film he's ever seen, except for in U2's *Rattle and Hum*, which he still can't bear thinking about.

What the fuck happened to those guys?!

"Okay, the best song about revolution," he says to himself. "Bad Religion's 'We're Only Gonna Die (How Could Hell Be Any Worse?).' You *have* to start off with that one! Even has *parentheses*!"

Vicky struggles to find her club footing. "I thought you were quiet and shy and not worthy of my attention, and here you are, the secret and powerful voice of grunge Seattle!" *another theme*

"I could *always* communicate," says Skip. "It just had to be behind a microphone. But no longer."

"Do you still have to talk through your voice decoder?" asks Willow.

"I do not—" Skip clears his throat. He turns off the voice decoder. He feels naked now. "No, I do not."

248

"You were DJ Truth all along!" says Vicky, head dripping with Surge. *DJ truth all along*

"All along," agrees Skip. "DJ Truth was Skip. And Skip was DJ Truth. We're one and the same. Now, no more hiding."

"What is it you want?" Tabitha asks, mic thrust before Skip's mouth. "Why did you come out of the shadows like that? Are you the *devil*?"

"I want my store back," announces Skip. "I want it the way it was before."

"One problem," says a voice.

"Oh no," says Willow.

"Oh boy," says Vicky. She's afraid to look but feels she must.

It's Mr. Straight.

"And that problem would be … can you guess?" asks Mr. Straight. "*Right*. That I *own* your store. As well as all the other stores now in this failing strip mall. And as you can see," he says, pointing to the thousands of suburbanites holding up signs in favor of his new store, "I have a few fans."

"Why don't we take it to our viewers?" asks Tabitha.

"Take what?" asks Toody. "*Takewhaaaaatttttt?!!!!! Not followinggggg!! Not the smartest!*"

"The choice," says Tabitha. "Let's take it to our viewers."

And then to Mister Loder, Tabitha says: "Take it to the viewers."

Mister Loder sighs. "Fine. I'll *take it* to the viewers."

"You can't do that!" says Mr. Straight. "I *own* this building! This building is *mine*! There is no decision but my *own*!"

"Not so fast," says Spooner, slapping a shot into a makeshift net and missing. He blades around the small group. He pats his messenger's bag looped over his shoulder.

"Do you know what's in here?" Spooner asks. "I'll tell you. Within this bag is an exceedingly important document from a local businessman to a certain Seattle mayor with the requisite forms that prove ownership of a certain strip mall. *Never* delivered it," continues Spooner, laughing. "My bad!" *lazy spooner*

He blades off, performing a figure zero. *becomes a hero*

"Are you fucking *serious*?" asks Mr. Straight. "You fucking idiot! All of you! *Morons*! All of you are goddamn *idiots*!"

He points to Toody. He points to Spooner. He points to Wake and to Bake and to Jack Jack and Becca and Mac. He points to Cody and Wes and to Royce.

He stops pointing.

"We may be idiots," says Toody. "But—"

He pauses.

He finishes: "We may be idiots."

"What is it with you and your friends?!" Mr. Straight screams to Willow. "I mean, what is your *purpose*? *All of you*?! You guys are *useless*!"

Willow straightens her back and launches into a speech she's been waiting to give for more than a week now. "Our *purpose*? I'll tell you what our purpose is *not*. It's to *not* end up in a suburban house,

250

with a wasteful lawn and a plastic fence to keep out those *scary* urban invaders. With your blue BMWs and easy-listening Muzak. With your bright, shiny clothing and your *easy* answers. Like lambs to the slaughter you all march out of your pens and into the killing fields, without a sound, without complaint. But I will *not* do that!"

"My BMW is red," says Mr. Straight. "And I don't listen to Muzak. I listen to Paul Simon."

Willow goes on: "You can take your eighty-hour work weeks and *stuff* them! You can take your Nike shoes and run straight into the hills with them!"

"I have Adidas—"

"You can take your *red* Beemers and drive off a cliff with them! It's time for a *fresh* generation to do what the Boomers never could! It's up to us to clean this capitalistic mess! Fellow graduates … *suck on my tasty lethargy*!"

Willow flashes the victory sign and waits for the applause to arrive.

It does not.

A loud cry is heard emanating from up on the roof.

It's Wes.

"Dad! Mom!" he screams.

Beneath him, about twelve feet to the ground, stand two middle-aged parents.

"You've arrived!" Wes says. "I *knew* you would! My protest *worked*!"

"Come on down, son," proclaims Wes's father. "We've had enough of this foolishness."

"We love you, Wesley," says Wes's mother.

"Wesley, we love you very much."

Like all mothers of homosexuals in 1990s movies, Margaret insists on using her son's full birth name. "We don't care *what* you are, Wesley! Even if it's of this new homosexual persuasion. Isn't that right, Howard?"

Wes's father grumbles.

"*What*?" Wes's mother asks. "Isn't that *right*, Howard?!"

"Fine, *yes*, sure, I don't *know*."

"What?!" Margaret asks, louder.

"Yes! Yes! *Fine, Martha*! We're just fine with our son being a ... *homo-shexual*!" *before people under- stood gays*

Like all fathers of homosexuals in 1990s movies, Howard insists on mispronouncing "homosexual."

It's all so strangely endearing.

"Good," says Margaret. "Then come on down, Wesley. We are ready for you now!"

Gingerly, Wes slides off the roof and onto the pavement. His knees buckle. He's still wearing his graduation robe, which is now practically deteriorating into dust spores.

The Seattle weather has truly taken its toll on this outfit.

"We love you *whoever* you are, *wherever* you choose to sit," says Wes's mother, helping him stand. "And we'd like to introduce you to someone very, very special. He was sitting on the sloped roof of daddy's S&L bank. Daddy thought ... well, daddy thought you just might enjoy each other's ... *company*."

"It was *your* idea, Margaret," hisses Howard.

"Not *mine*."

"With a *tiny* bit of encouragement from me," admits Margaret.

"I only told you that another man's son was sitting on my roof," mumbles Charles. "To protest. That's all I said, Margaret."

It's been a rough month for Howard. On top of his S&L failing, his only son has been sitting on a sloped roof for two weeks to protest ... *what exactly?*

He doesn't know.

Now, even worse, cable TV has arrived to cover it for all the world to see.

Really, this the last thing the jury in Howard's ongoing fraud, racketeering and conspiracy trial needs to witness, all of them sequestered back in a Best Western in Nebraska.

Jesus, he's tired.

"We thought that you might ... *enjoy* each other's company," continues Margaret. "This is Chadley. Chadley, Wes."

Wes sizes up his roof-sitting doppelganger. *Doesn't appear too bad. A bit disheveled, yes. But that's okay.*

Chad, too, is wearing a ratty graduation robe and a mortar board. "Chad," he mumbles. "Not Chadley."

"Bend," says Wes.

"Bend?" asks Chad.

"Bend. So I can see what's written on your mortar board."

Chad does as he's told. Atop his graduation hat, in white electrical tape is written, "NOW?!"

It's Wes's turn to bend. "And *my* hat," he says,

"reads WHAT."

"Well, weren't you two *made* for each other?" says Margaret, beaming. "Together you read 'WHAT NOW'! Right, Howard?"

"Right, dear," says Howard. *God, he looks exhausted.*

"*Right*, Howard?!" Margaret asks again, louder.

"YES, DEAR!" Howard cries.

What did he do to deserve all this? Besides ripping off millions from his fellow parishioners?

Margaret smiles. *So it's settled then!*

Cody blinks out "This is so cool!" And then, "Honestly, I could really use the pillow flipped again!"

Margaret points to Cody lying on the rented hospital bed. "And who would this be? One of your … *friends*?"

"Yes," says Wes. "One of the Lost Boys. He communicates with blinks."

"Wonderful," Wes's father says. "Most *wonderful*, indeed."

An explosion occurs just next to the stage.

The crowd, at first frightened, now cheers wildly.

"What's happening?" asks Willow.

"The show is about to start!" exclaims Tabitha. "The Great American Grunge Off!"

"Start?" asks Toody, confused. "But my palms are sore! From slapping!"

"Get up there," says Willow. "This is your one chance!"

"Willow, we need to talk first," says Toody.

"Now?!"

"Yeah, *now*. *This* way."

Toody leads Willow off to the side, stroking his "grunge sponge," just 'neath his lower lip. Tonight it's in the shape of a perfectly-formed frowny face. He readjusts his foam ear plug in his right nostril.

Miraculously, somehow it's managed to remain lodged throughout the fight.

"Willow, I want to tell you something. And it's important."

"Yes?"

"I wanted to tell you that I never did sleep with that woman from the other night, I'm … forgetting her name. Courtney? Kat? I can't remember."

"The syphilitic penis?"

"You really have to trust me, Willow. I've *never* slept with a syphilitic penis! A syphilitic *vagina*, well …" He grows quiet and sad.

"Toody, you've had a few days to think about what I asked before. So I'm going to ask again: *what exactly am I to you*?"

"You're my Willow," Toody says, and smiles. "You know that, don't you? Just … good ol' Willow!"

Willow goes to turn but Toody grabs her and laughs.

"I'm just *teasing*, Willow! You're my *everything*! I would *never* have gotten this far without you!"

"We wanted to start a revolution," says Willow.

Toody shrugs. Apparently, he doesn't remember this. He just assumed it was all about the outdoor sex at Jimi Hendrix's gravesite.

"I guess we did," he says slowly, improvising.

"Yes, we did," Willow declares. "But you were more concerned with your own quest to perform the world's most perfect stage dive than worry about *my* own personal quest. To capture my generation on a Fuji DS-100 digicam with 3-power zoom and a 10-byte flash-memory card."

"*Whaaaaaaa*?" asks Toody, arms dramatically spread.

"You just don't get it," says Willow.

Toody shakes his head. "I do, Willow. Look around you."

"Why?"

"Tell me what you see."

Willow looks into the distance. "Herpes Simplex One fucking Herpes Simplex Two next to a Dumpster?"

"No, I mean, *look* at us!" Toody goes into a deep crouch and a half-sit, one leg spread before him. He grabs an imaginary microphone stand: "Hello, Cleveland! Are you listening?! Here stands the most powerful couple on the entire Earth planet! *Toody* and *Willow*!"

He laughs very hard.

It's not particularly funny and Willow knows it, but Willow goes along with the non-mirth by giving a quick, fake laugh. It's really the easiest way to just end it.

But she thinks: *Could what Toody is now incoherently mumbling possibly be true?*

Is this idiot actually speaking the truth for the first time ever, even by accident or brain-damaged mistake?

Could Toody actually be ... inadvertently wise?

Toody holds out his hands towards Willow.

Should she accept it?

"Together again?" Toody asks like a child. "Toody and Willow, *together again*?"

Toody's "I'M A LOSER (YEAH, RIGHT!)" fore-arm tattoo practically sparkles.

Why shouldn't she take his hand? She and Toody are what Willow's PSYCH 101 professor might have called "simpatico." Then again, the professor was referring to sociopathic men in prisons and the delusional women who love them.

Should she take it? she asks herself again. *Accept his hand?*

"Toody, I—"

Toody grunts, bends, and rips out a low one. His fart is in the key of D.

Even passing gas in Seattle these days must be dropped in the key of D.

Toody's eyes are closed, a trait he's infamous for while deeply and truly enjoying his own odor.

"You haven't changed a bit, Toody," Willow exclaims. She doesn't even bother for an apology. She knows it will never arrive.

She's *still* waiting for the fart apology from their first dinner date at the Sizzler in Matthews Beach.

The table next to theirs had mistakenly thought the food had arrived early.

"Maybe," Toody says, eyes still closed. "Maybe not. But what I'm saying is that we're a team. And we should *stick together*. As a team."

"You still have so much growing up to do," Willow says. "You can't stay like this forever. Will you ever be able to talk without a distortion box?"

"Yes," he says, through the distortion box.

"Just get up there and perform," says Willow.

"I will," says Toody. "But can you give me an answer? Toody and Willow? Together again?

"Maybe," says Willow. "I … I have to think about it."

"I knew it!" says Toody, hugging himself. "Guys! Let's hit it! The stage!"

That's Your Problem, minus Toody, take to the flimsy pressed-wood stage and grab all of the instruments that they would be playing if only they were able.

There's a hush from the crowd.

A flickering strobe lights turn on.

All four band members are standing stock still.

Tad, Tad, Tad and Tad.

The strobe lights are accomplishing nothing.

Toody emerges from out of the backstage wings, like the grunge star he was bred to be.

The crowd, evenly divided amongst those wanting to keep the store open and those wanting to have it closed, join together to rock out before MTV's powerful cameras.

They can disagree later. Now it's time to show the world what they're made of: *Seattle Oak*.

Without hesitation, and as if he's been waiting for this bizarre moment his entire life, Toody gets down into a sprinter's crouch.

"Ten," he says.

Jesus, thinks Willow. *Do we have to sit through an entire countdown?*

"Nine," he continues.

Just get on with it!

"Eight."

Willow could use a daydream. Should she call 1-900-DAY-DREA? Where's Tabitha's cellular IBM Simon telephone?

"Seven."

"Just do it!" screams someone from the crowd.

Toody smiles.

He just does it.

He breaks into a jog, which becomes a slow trot, and it's then that he takes off from the stage ... straight into the now unified audience!

It is a thing of beauty: an extension of the arms, soaring like a Doc Martined bird, falling quickly, caught by the crowd, a glance up, as if to the grunge heavens above, a flip over like a dung beetle, legs flexing and re-flexing, being carried back to the stage like a fallen Messiah to re-enact it all over again, a scrambling onstage, the beginning of yet another countdown, being yelled at to just get on with it already, crouching into yet another sprinter's crouch, about to again take wobbly flight after a slow trot—

The crowd awaits anxiously.

No. He's finished.

Toody exits the stage.

Flickering strobe lights turn off.

"There he goes," says the woman next to Willow, excitedly. "There goes *Toody*!"

The band drop their instruments, the ones they'd play if only they could, and exit. Years from now, one will overdose; one will be murdered; one will commit suicide; and one will open a high-end umbrella store in the U district.

"He did okay," admits Vicky.

"*More* than okay," says Willow. "*Very* okay. And he's worked super hard for this!"

"Even at the expense of your relationship," says Vicky.

Leave it to the mediocre-looking woman to tell the truth!

"Willow. Hi."

Willow turns.

It's Toody, back from his amazing performance. He's covered in performance sweat. Willow wonders if the sweat is even real. Oftentimes he'll just spray himself with mineral water.

"You did real *wood*, Tood!" exclaims Willow.

It's their own private language. Also, it rhymes.

Barely.

"Huh?" asks Toody. And then, pressing the foot pedal on his distortion box, his voice becomes even more distorted: "*Huh? What you say?*"

"You did real well," enunciates Willow slowly.

"I don't …" he starts. He appears more confused than is typical.

Maybe Toody has once again forgotten their own private language? Yet one more gorgeous global language lost for all eternity!

"When's the next band coming on?" asks Willow to Tabitha.

"They're not. That was it," says Tabitha. "The results from the polls are back."

"That was *fast!*" says Vicky.

"Call-in polls," says Tabitha. "The latest trend!"

"Well?" asks Willow.

"First, the results of the Grunge Off."

"Did I win?" asks Toody. "Did I?"

"Do any of you in the band even play instruments?" asks Tabitha.

"My *body* is my instrument," says Toody. "And I often *play* with it. So that works, right?"

"It doesn't, no. But you're very attractive. So it doesn't matter."

They nod. Tabitha has a point. Toody really is dumber than a flounder on a bed of ice in Chinatown and about just as talented.

But he *is* extremely attractive, no one can argue that.

Tabitha goes on: "So, it looks like Toody and his band won. Then again, they were the only band performing— or pretending to."

Toody beams.

"Now, as far as the record store, sixty-eight percent of those around the world would *love* for Skip to once again run his store into the ground! Twenty-two percent would *prefer* for Mr. Straight to continue to run the new store in its current modernistic capacity. Ten percent just want to see more footage of Toody with his shirt off."

"So I can have my store back?" asks Skip.

"That's what America would prefer," says Tabitha. "Make that, the *world*."

Skip's eyes are tearing. Whether it's from gratitude or the infection from reading too many liner notes, he won't soon know.

"I suppose," Skip declares. "I suppose I *have* won. But I now own a store with a lice-free listening station. I never wanted *that* in life. All I ever wanted was to annoy customers with my toxic love for bands that so few can tolerate."

"Maybe it is a sign," says Willow. "To *change* with a *changing* city. Take the best of the current store and make it into your own."

"But will they love me as DJ Truth or just plain old Skip?" asks Skip.

Vicky goes to answer but before she can, a man's voice is heard.

"Not so fast!"

It's a familiar voice.

"Oh no," says Willow.

"Oh boy," says Vicky. She's afraid to look but feels she must.

It's Mr. Straight, of course.

"You *disappoint* me, Willow."

Willow stands tall. No bigger than a wisp but sturdier than anything that could possibly stand in her way. More than merely beautiful … beautifully *obtainable*.

"Yeah? How so?"

"How I wanted to give you the good life," Mr. Straight says. "How very much I wanted to give you everything that you'd ever would have needed. Instead you …" He looks around. "Wanted *this*. Whatever *this* is. Enjoy. Have a great life. With your … *dinky* friends."

He waits for the reaction.

Of which there is none.

"I said, 'Have a great life!'" says Mr. Straight.

"We heard you," says Willow, sharply. "Go blast your post-colonialist Paul Simon out of your blue mechanical asshole."

"It's not a mechanical asshole," he says. "And it's *red*."

"Actually, *you're* the asshole," says Trust Exercise Ben.

He's been here all along.

"You're fired," says Mr. Straight to his assistant.

"Actually, *you're* fired," says Trust Exercise Ben. "It's *my* company now."

"And why would that be, shit for brains?"

"Because of *this*," says Ben, pulling out a sheaf of papers. "Papers that prove that you … did something wrong … at the company."

It's not specific but it appears to work.

The crowd gasps.

"You bastard!"

"Papers that will prove … you aren't nearly the successful businessman you claim to be," Ben goes on.

"Let me see those papers!" screams Mr. Straight.

263

I FUCKING HATE STEWART!!

"Where did you get those?!"

"Trust games," says Ben. "*You* trusted *me*. And that was your undoing. It's time for me to take over. I'll work with companies to help *improve* them. It'll be a ... symbiosis. It'll be *non*-aggressive. A new, gentler time shall be arriving in 1993!"

"I'm not done," announces Mr. Straight. "Oh, I'm not done at all!"

Why exactly is Mr. Straight being replaced in his own company?

Only Ben knows the answer to this question.

And the screenwriter.

Both aren't talking.

"How much realistically," says Topper, skate-boarding past Jack Jack. "How much realistically to go pitch a dig ol' stinky on Mr. Straight's blue Beemer?"

"*Red*," says Mr. Straight. "And you're not pitching a dig ol' stinky anywhere."

"I'd do that for free," says Jack Jack. "I would do that for *more* than free. I'd fucking pay *you*."

His hobo hat flutters in the slight breeze.

"You'll do nothing of the sort," exclaims Mr. Straight, rushing over to his BMW. The crowd—the entire crowd, even those earlier rooting for him—now taunt him.

"Hang on," says Tabitha. "C'mere."

"Why?" asks Mr. Straight.

"Not you," Tabitha says. "*You*" (she points to Willow) "and you" (pointing to Toody) "and you" (pointing to Skip). "*All* of you. Follow me."

Tabitha stops and turns.

264

"And (pointing to Mr. Straight) *you* can go."

The crowd again laughs.

"Bastards," Mr. Straight mutters. "I'll own you *all* soon enough."

"Optimist!" someone hisses.

Mr. Straight starts the engine, turns on *Graceland* full blast. The thumping, *awee-ahaway* rhythms of South African Soweto music strained so awkwardly through the aura of 1950s Queens, New York doo-wop, pulsates for all to hear.

"*Rabid dingo*," says Royce. "Rabid dingo go *bye-bye*."

Mr. Straight does, indeed, go bye-bye.

Willow, walking next to Skip, shakes her head: "Good riddance!"

"*Harsh* realm, dipshit!" announces Skip.

Willow laughs for what seems like the first time in hours. *Theme. Prof. Doherty says in the movie*

"Skip! You're talking like a grunger now!" *they cry*

"Maybe we're ... *all* grungers," says Skip wisely.

"You know, I was supposed to fire you," she says to Skip. "He wanted me to fire you from your own store."

"I figured as much. So why didn't you?"

"I *love* you, Skip. And I only want what's best for you. You're the only boss I've ever had. Plus, you disappeared, only to re-emerge as someone walking down a mysterious hill in shadow."

"I'm not used to real emotions," Skip says. "I'm twenty-nine years old, for crying out loud, and I'm not used to human affection."

"Neither am I," says Willow. "Neither are any

265

of us! That's our generation! But let's try to change that! *Together*!"

Vicky runs up to Skip. She grabs his hand.

"You don't mind, do you? If I *hold* your hand?" Vicky asks Skip, more shyly than Willow has ever heard her friend speak.

"I don't," Skip says, smiling. "At all. Top five songs about falling in love—" he starts and then stops. "You know what? No more lists. Gonna stop making lists and I'm gonna … start making *love*."

He blushes but still pulls Vicky in closer—or as closely as he can with her medical shoes blocking the way.

"Okay," says Tabitha, sitting in a director's chair, propping her feet on Kurt Loder's back. "Here's what we have. We have *you* (pointing to Skip) who still owns the record store. We have them (pointing to Cody and Topper) who still run the video store and In-Convenience Mart. And we have you (pointing to Willow) who wants to be the documentarian voice of her generation."

"Have you watched the footage yet?" Willow asks, anxiously.

"Yes."

"And? …"

"It was garbage."

Willow now feels like Mr. Straight must have when she told him his mixed tape was terrible. *It's not a good feeling.* "I worked *hard* on that."

"Here's what I propose," says Tabitha, ignoring Willow. "MTV is looking for garbage. But just that

266

right type of garbage."

Kurt Loder shifts position beneath Tabitha to provide for maximum comfort.

"I propose that we create our own reality."

"I don't understand," says Willow. "I already shot my own reality."

"Yours," says Tabitha. "Now I want you to shoot *our* reality. The *true* reality."

"Which is what exactly?" asks Willow.

"I'll have a script for you tomorrow morning," Tabitha says.

"A *script*?" asks Willow.

"A *script*?" repeats Skip.

"Willow," says Tabitha, "you and Toody might love each other but you might not. You go back and forth."

"True," says Willow.

"Skip and Vicky, you just fell in love. Skip was DJ Truth. No one knew until tonight. So is Vicky falling in love with DJ Truth or Skip?"

"We still don't understand," says Willow, speaking for all of them. "Is this for real?"

"Real?" asks Tabitha. "What's *real*? Create your own *real*. Right, Mr. Loder?"

"Right," the fifty-six-year-old answers, on all fours, miserable. "*Right*."

"You've *all* won tonight," says Tabitha. "Trust me on this."

Tabitha pulls out her IBM Simon. She dials.

Kurt, beneath her, answers on his own IBM Simon. This is the second of these three honeys in the world.

"Hello?"

"Move a little to the left please."

"Okay."

Tabitha hangs up. So does Kurt.

"That just cost me $45. Let's get started."

They get started.

Homework
- biopaper
- weekly response
- something else I can't remember...

The Following Tuesday, 3:57 P.M.

The Number One VINYL Music Express, renamed and reconfigurated for the second time, is packed.

It's the world premiere of *Reality World: Seattle*. The episode is airing on MTV and playing on five large television screens scattered around the store— and throughout the world.

Skip takes a look around. *Gosh, it's been a long seven days!*

The shoot has been going on non-stop since Tabitha first announced her plans for the show.

And they've accomplished *so* much.

More than that, the record store has returned to its alternative roots.

But with a few tiny improvements.

The lice-ridden listening station has returned—but with a can of Lysol.

The back office has reverted to its original mess, covered floor to ceiling with that perfect amount of music-related chaos: concert ticket stubs from local clubs pinned to corkboards; promotional album sleeves of the most recent releases of local bands with names that sound familiar but not overly; an extremely hilarious funny rubber chicken nailed above the bathroom door; stacks of cassettes leaning *this* way and *that*.

The NOW PLAYING sign has remained digital but it's been updated to reflect Skip's *true* tastes:

UP NEXT: XTC *Skylarking*!

The CD is on pause, just itching for "Dear God" to begin.

Meanwhile, the first episode of what they've worked on for the last week unfurls.

It all takes place within "The Reality House," built just for this show. Six levels, ten bathrooms, a video camera hidden in every crack and crevice, missing nothing.

Word has it the house was erected next to the one that used to be owned by Seattle native Bruce Lee himself!

Or Jimi Hendrix. No one can remember.

The *Reality World: Seattle* gang consists of:

Willow, 23, who has flown to Seattle from back east to capture her generation on shaky video. She's an incredible young, fresh talent!

"Trying reading Charles Bukowski!" Willow screams inside the house's living room. "It just might do you some good*!"*

Toody, 24, lives inside the attic. He wants to be the world's most famous grunge singer, after Kurt. Will he ever be able to hook up with his best friend from high school and form a bond that will benefit the *both* of them?

"All I [beep] want to do is write the [beep] world's first grunge opera?! Is that too hard!" half-screams Toody in the kitchen of the group house.

Toody still likes Willow. But does Willow like Toody back? Will Toody ever apologize after farting? *Can they make it work?!* Toody's soul patch—with the help of some professional MTV styling—is now in the perfectly-formed shape of a dollar sign.

It will soon become a "thing."

Vicky, 22, is a live cannon, considered attractive but not in the "traditional" sense. She helps her older boyfriend, Skip, manage his singular, alternative record store. Vicky just loves to dress Toby the Wonder Dog each morning as a different, real-life feminist hero.

This particular episode, Toby is dressed as Andrea Dworkin.

The small pair of overalls is adorable.

Mac is 21. He is a strict Buddhist who once high-fived the Dalai Lama. He's in love with Becca, 23, who owns Seattle's only all-flannel condom and IUD female-positive sex store. They both are in love with *love.*

"I [beep] hate you!" screams Mac, on screen.

"And I [beep] despise you!" screams Becca, on screen. "All I want to do is see Matt Dillon in a terrible grunge wig! That's all I [beep] want!!!!!!!!!!!"

The crowd watching within the record store screams with pleasure.

Mac and Becca give each other a high five.

It's all in good fun. This *reality has no bearing on the* other.

It's all a lie but that's okay. You're only what people are told you are.

Become what you're not. Easy. It's a new age.

Cody, 22, is a workaholic and the owner of Video Plus, the newest and most modern video store in all Seattle. It even has a Drive-Thru! In addition to movies featuring Julia Roberts running from the Supreme Court with a sheaf of papers held high in the air, the store also rents videos that feature white teachers bestowing upon minority inner-city youth their great white wisdom.

Even more exciting, it's rumored that the video store will one day soon carry "Digital Versatile Discs."

That stands for "D.V.D."

"Give me back my [beep] fanny pack!" screams Cody on screen, drunk and taking a swing at someone off screen. "My dick is a goddamn lethal weapon!"

Topper, 21, is the owner of the Super Convenient Shopping Boutique & Market, a high-end store that only sells the purest and healthiest food options in all of Seattle.

There will even soon be a roasted chicken "nook."

"I don't know about pain?! I don't know about sadness?!" screams Topper in the reality house's kitchen. "I lost my library card because of [beep] excessive fines! How do I not know about [beep] sadness?!"

Spooner, 23, is the roller-blading champion of Seattle, five years running. He's training to win it *again* this year!

"I've got to train harder!" he screams in the house's large library that contains no books. "This is for all the gold! They're gunning for me, man!"

Jack Jack, the owner of the city's first chain of sensory deprivation-tank stores (Altered Fates), offers free sessions for any returning Iraq War vets suffering from post-traumatic stress syndrome. He's a local hero and plans to soon meet with the mayor very soon to perform his conceptual one-person show about the Rodney King Situation during a seventh-inning stretch at the Kingdome during the All-Star game.

He's hoping to make a very important point about race relations.

Bake, 20, sleeps all day, every day, in a hammock in the backyard of the group house. His one goal in life is to be featured as a "Premiere Seller" on QVC so that he can hawk his hand-crafted, ceramic, artis-anal bongs. The MTV cameras will be tagging along tomorrow morning for his phenomenal pitch!

Wes and Chad are in love with each other, but will Chad remain faithful to Wes while off on tour with Blues Traveler, working as John Popper's harmonica tech?

Royce—just back from the Gulf War where he received the Purple Heart for incredible bravery—is a successful graffiti tagger and inventor of the brand-new "Grunge Font," hired by restaurants and clubs to "grunge up" their businesses.

"I swear I'll tag 'Mayhem' against the side of the [beep] White House wall or [beep] die trying!" screams Royce.

Last, and not to be forgotten, is Mr. Straight, who is *also* a character on *Reality World: Seattle*.

Tabitha, at the last minute, changed her mind.

"I love sex!" screams Mr. Straight on screen. *"I don't care who I have it with! Sex is good! Like greed is good! Sex and greed are good!"*

Mr. Straight is 26 and older than the rest, except for Skip, and generally hated. He's a very successful Businessman who plans to open the city's only clinic for men of a certain age.

It's the most up-to-date way to treat impotence and probably will be for decades.

"It's a solid-ass investment! I can't lose!" he says *from the house's backyard porch that overlooks the outdoor fire pit. "One shot and you're hot!"*

In the record store, Mr. Straight now gives Willow a look. *Why did he get so upset before? There are plenty of women to bang!* He winks. She ignores him. *But no hard feelings, right? Especially now that they're both TV stars!*

By the time the episode finishes—with Willow screaming at Vicky for not cleaning the sink properly, with Toody just about to head out on a date with a professional indoor cheerleader for a professional lacrosse league, with Vicky screaming at Skip for forgetting their one-day anniversary, with Cody promoting his new video store on a TV ad by using his ass cheeks as a ventriloquist dummy—and after the applause dies down and after the entire cast starts drinking and laughing and commenting on Mister Loder working behind the bar and looking miserable, and after they have a conversation about how different TV reality is from actual *true* reality—bigger, more fun, somehow more *true,* more compliant to whatever your dream happens to be—and how all their lives will soon change drastically for the better—the sun has finally set, and the party goes on through the night, cameras not missing a thing, capturing it *all* for the upcoming second episode of this new hit show that deals with reality.

Meanwhile, outside the store, from his perch against the wall, Wake makes not a sound. He's been here all night.

Mute as always, Wake notices a white stretch enter the lot.

It parks just next to him, engine revving.

One of the back windows rolls down.

"Where is everyone?"

It's Brendan Bryant.

On either side of him sit two men, slightly older. Wake shrugs.

"Still not talking, I see," says Brendan, squeezing a hacky sack with the colors of the South African flag.

It's not subjugation, these colors. It's respect!

Wake nods in the affirmative. He notices that Brendan no longer sports a derby hat or carries with him a cherry wood cane with a gold eagle on the tip.

Just a striped Oxford button-down.

"Wake, I'd like you to meet two of my very dear friends," says Brendan. "This is *Steve* and this is *Jeff*."

Wake nods to both. They, too, are wearing striped Oxford button-downs, fully buttoned.

Maybe it's a new look?

"We're headed to Palo Alto and then maybe back up to Seattle. To *change* the world."

Wake remains silent.

"There's an entire new reality out there, Wake," Brendan says. "But I think you already *know* that."

Wake touches one finger to his forehead.

"Is that code?" asks Brendan.

Another finger to Wake's forehead.

"A yes?"

One tap.

"Then a yes. You're really not so dumb after all," says Brendan. "Just … a bit choosy about what you say aloud. And maybe a little socially … *off*."

One tap.

"I think you'll fit in very well with us. You have some *ideas*, don't you? For the *future*."

Wake nods.

"Would you care to join us?"

One tap.

"Or would you care to stay behind at these …" Brendan glances around, "… retail establishments and their abandoned pup tents? This pre-modernistic take on the future? Surrounded by people who have no idea that there's a door beyond the door? And doors endlessly beyond that, leading into forever?"

One tap from Wake.

"But you always knew that."

One tap.

"Get in then," says Brendan, smiling. "Maybe it's just time you get in."

"Yes," says Wake. "I think I will."

"Whoa! He *talks*!" screams the driver, Jessica. "My god in heaven above! He actually *talks*!"

"Yes," says Wake. "I *talk*."

"You always did, you sly dog," says Jennifer, more gorgeous then ever.

"He *always* did," Brendan repeats, smiling. "I'll be *damned*."

Wake opens the front passenger door and enters. He turns and nods to the two in the back, this *Jeff* and this *Steve*, and he takes the seat next to this gorgeous Jessica.

The two new men say nothing. Not the chatty types, necessarily, but filled with *tons* of interesting ideas.

Wake has a feeling they're all going to become good friends.

"Let's hit it," he says.

"Wake says let's hit it," says Brendan. "So let's hit it *hard*!"

Imagine floating up through thick, yeasty clouds and observing a stretch limousine heading out of a city pulsating with youth. Keep floating towards the heavens, past the towers, through the mist, and you will soon come to realize that this is the most exciting time in history to be young and alive. The rain-soaked streets vibrate with an intensity that can barely be described. There's anguish. Pain. All deliciously mixed into a sludgy gumboed sluice spiced with a dash of angst and a pinch of torment.

This is Seattle.

This is the early 1990s.

It is *exhilarating*.

A blue Volvo with Connecticut license plates enters

277

the parking lot as the white-stretch limo is exiting.

Willow's parents.

Is their daughter still working at this mall, like she once told them? Or has she moved overseas? The FBI would love to talk with her! Credit card fraud. For an Exxon card her father never even owned! Up to half a million! Also, for hacking into his 401K and stealing nearly all of it!

"*Look*," says Willow's father. "That must be the goddamn telephone that was always being answered by the jackass asking for the definition for irony."

"I wonder if he ever learned it?"

"If not, he just *might*."

"Pull over," Willow's mother says. "And let's see what the hell is going on … here in this … *shit hole*."

Limitless, the possibilities, the beginning of an entire generation of astonishing achievements.

Grunge.

Apathy.

Trucker hats with YOUR LOGO HERE.

The car pulls over and idles. *Should they get out? Place looks filthy.*

And sad.

The car remains idling, smoke billowing.

Papers and fast-food trash circle in the slight breeze—lifting high into the air—as if inserted by 1991-era computer special effects.

It is all very poetic.

A magic that will last forever. And this is where our astonishing story comes to a moisty and logy end.

Until the following year, when all characters up

and move to Austin.
    Seattle is fucking done.

THE END

Prof. Doherty 'Read
Stinker Lets Loose' watch
movies w/ different themes then
this one more bout having fun
not isolation but just having fun
like Passable in Pink takes place
in 1982 jim hughs director...

Don't forget to
do your weekly responses...
fuck it. I dont read them
anyways.

NOW! YOU CAN ORDER
Sunshine Beam Publishing BY MAIL!

Here are some suggestions from
Sunshine Beam's MOVIE TIE-IN LIBRARY:

- [ ] **V101** Odd Boy Who Blows Raspberries
- [ ] **V102** Ain't No Dung Heap High Enough
- [ ] **V103** The Space Monkey Who Fell From the Sky and Caused Havoc
- [x] **V104** Dirty Tricky Bicycle Daredevils
- [ ] **V105** Giants of Professional Tickling
- [ ] **V106** Chucky Esposito on Mars
- [x] **V107** Chucky Esposito in the Canyon of Death
- [x] **V108** Stinker Strikes Back
- [x] **V109** Stinker Goes All In
- [ ] **V110** D.A.V.E., Intergalactic Toll Taker
- [ ] **V111** Disco Conspiracy II
- [ ] **V112** Smelly Mists of Glover
- [x] **V113** Wicked Lovin' Back Kisses
- [x] **V114** ALIVE: The Story of the Epcot Centre Survivors
- [ ] **V115** Rascal Eat Baby
- [ ] **V116** Satin Shenanigans
- [ ] **V117** Rollerskating Rabbi
- [ ] **V118** The Caramel-Flavored Popcorn Wars
- [ ] **V119** M.C. Higgins, the Tricky Country'Coon
- [ ] **V120** Alcoholic Rich Man Who Wears a Top Hat While in Hot Tub
- [ ] **V121** The Candied-Apple Gang
- [ ] **V122** The Boy Who Could Make Himself Appear
- [ ] **V123** Return to Crumb Mountain

Please send me the books I have checked.

Enclose check or money order only, no cash please. Allow $1.99 for each book plus 50¢ per copy to cover postage and handling. N.Y. State residents add applicable sales tax.

Please allow 2 weeks for delivery.

SUNSHINE BEAM PUBLISHING
P.O. BOX 762142
Hollywood, CA 90072

Name MARY COOPER

Address 12918 River Road

City Poolesville   State MD   Zip 20837

HI-RIZE BOOK CASES

The ALL-IN-ONE Solution to Your ALL-IN-EVERYTHING Paperback Book Storage Problem

YOU LOVE YOUR PAPERBACK BOOKS.

Who wouldn't. But they deserve a good and proper home that is free from dirt, diapers and felines.

Save valuable shelf space; keep paperback books for ever and ever; an attractive addition to any living room; available in avocado green and golden-streamed yellow; plants well in all shag carpeting; padded leatherette covering complements any room décor.

CHOICE OF TWO COLORS:
001 avocado green / 002 golden-streamed yellow

- These stackable shelves tilt back to prevent books from losing lustre.
- Handsome outer case elegantly embossed in expensive appearing faux gold leaf
- Alphebetized professional-type library stickers to avoid confusion and time waiting.

$9⁹⁵ EA

Stores app. 15 books
ITEM No. 32478

1-900-DAY-DREA

Too lazy to daydream?!
Let the daydream come to you!

WANNA DAYDREAM BUT DON'T HAVE THE INI-
TIATIVE? CALL 1-900-DAY-DREA AND LET US
COME UP WITH THE IDEAS FOR YOU!

*Popularity Daydreams!	*Realistic Daydreams!
*Sex Daydreams!	*Pscychdeic Daydreams!
*Romantic Daydreams!	*Sporty Daydreams!
*Adventure Daydreams!	*Business Daydreams!
*Fantasy Daydreams!	

IT'S ALL YOURS FOR THE PRICE OF A SINGLE
FEW QUARTERS! OUR WELL-TRAINED OPERATORS ARE
STANDING BY AND WAITING TO HELP!

"OUTRAGEOUS BARGAIN! AS
THE TERMINATOR SAYS, I
WILL BE BACK! HEY — NOT
A BAD IDEA FOR A DAY-
DREAM!!"

Adult Daydreamers ONLY!

$2.25 the first minute. $1.50 minute each additional minute.